CHAPTER ONE

He had been driving for the better part of the day by now. These long and tedious drives pretty much forced him to reflect on his life, past, present and future.

He had come from a small family, just his parents and a younger sister. His father had been a workaholic and heavy drinker. His mother was a vague and withdrawn housewife. They had meant well, but the best way he could describe their parenting style was "benign neglect." He wasn't complaining. That suited him just fine. He took after his father, whom he admired for his relentless drive, discipline and independent nature. *I work hard. I pay the bills and I don't have to answer to anyone. People like me do just fine on our own. We don't need approval from anyone.*

He had always doted on his younger sister who was born just eleven months after him. From an early age, he had willingly become her protector. He had guarded and guided her through all of her significant life events. In return, his sister mothered him like their own mother never could. Not that he needed mothering, mind you, but it made Marjorie feel good and useful, so he let her do it. Their close sibling relationship was the great comfort in his life. He could always count on Marjorie. *Marjorie is the one person who never let me down.*

His father had died suddenly when he was in his first year of college. At nineteen, he became the head of the household, working his way through the last three years of his education, taking care of and providing for Marjorie and his mother. There was no other option.

When his mother died of cancer a few years later, he had already started a lucrative career and his sister was on a good path. She graduated from a local two-year college with honors. Both brother and sister transitioned seamlessly into a comfortable life without parents.

Yessiree, he was a lot like the old man. Only problem was, sometimes he couldn't slow down. He was hard driving and wound very tight. Sometimes, he had to let off steam. Nothing illegal of course, but booze, women and gambling did have a special place in his life.

On several occasions, he had taken extended trips to Las Vegas without telling his sister. A few of those retreats lasted for weeks. Man-oh-man, had he gotten some tongue lashings over that. *Cut me a break, Marjorie.*

Another thing he loved was the ladies, and they loved him, but he had a hard time keeping any type of serious relationship going. Not that he did anything wrong, exactly, but he just didn't have the time to give them the attention they wanted. *Alright, I'll have to work on that. I don't want to be single my whole life.*

For now, though, he was fairly happy with his life, especially his career. *Except for these long drives. I gotta do something about that. Driving all the time is killing me.*

He thought about the sales seminar that was his destination, and about the strenuous workload his boss dumped on him every week. He thrived on hard work and was very good at his job. His home company paid him very well and he was proud of his accomplishments. If he kept it up, he was on the fast track for promotions and a lot more zeroes in his paychecks. He worked hard and played hard and saw no reason on earth why he should change his lifestyle anytime soon. *In a few years, I'll slow down and then I'll find a nice girl and settle down. I've got time.*

For the previous hour or so, his mind had wandered into more mundane territory and he was becoming distracted and lethargic. That was the thing about these long drives, there was too much time to think.

As he cruised down the highway, feeling drowsy, he noticed that it was beginning to drizzle. He turned on his windshield wipers and turned the radio off. "Jesus Christ, this is one dark road. Can't they afford streetlights?"

His GPS had guided him onto this road and he was glad for a little respite from the hectic traffic on the interstate and nothing but trees on both sides of the road. He yawned over and over and felt his back aching as the repetitive beat of the windshield wipers began to lull him into drowsiness.

He passed a few signs but didn't pay much attention to them. The drizzle began to get heavier. *I have to get a room. I can't make it all night in this shitty weather.*

As he drove on in the rain, the howling wind and darkening night, a figure suddenly appeared in the middle of the road, directly in the path of his car. He pumped on the brakes and the car skidded forward. Time seemed to be suspended as he tried desperately to swerve and avoid the figure. But the figure, who he could now recognize was a man, continued to move into the path of the car. For a moment, he could see the look of wild-eyed terror on the man's face.

There was a loud thud when the car struck the man and another thud as the body flew over the top of the car. He shouted angrily, "Goddam! What the fuck?"

He slammed on the breaks and skidded several feet, just managing to maintain control of the car but still leaving tire tracks on the road. He got out, looked at the dent in the car's hood and raced back to where he had hit the man. There was no one in the road and no one alongside the road. He turned and looked again. *What have I done? What have I done? Where is he?*

He ran down the shoulder and looked in the grassy areas on the side of the highway. He couldn't find anyone. *I know I hit him. I have a big dent in the hood to prove it.*

He continued to walk up and down both sides of the road, looking everywhere for the man he'd hit. He questioned if his exhaustion and inattention had contributed to the accident and he suddenly became frantic with guilt. The man could be seriously injured or dead. As hard as he looked, he could find nothing. *Come on! He's got to be out here somewhere. Someone doesn't just walk away after they've been hit by a car.*

Abruptly, the hairs on the back of his neck stood up. He turned in quick circles, squinting into the darkness and the rain reflected in his car lights. He had a strange feeling that he wasn't alone, like he was being watched. He suddenly felt vulnerable and his body registered danger even as he tried to dismiss the feeling. He quickly went back to his car, got in, and locked the doors.

As he sat there, alongside the highway, the adrenalin began to wear off and he realized just how exhausted he really was. He'd known the long drive would be wearing on him, but now, coupled with the shock of what had just happened, it was making him feel almost completely drained. *I have to stop somewhere for the night and I'll deal with this in the morning.*

He put the car in drive and slowly pulled away, watching obsessively in the rearview mirror for any kind of movement. *I know I hit someone. I know I did. I wasn't dreaming. I heard it. I saw it. I know I did.*

From behind the brush alongside the road, a man watched. He was stunned and slightly bloody, but he was alive. He would just stay where he was for a while and think about what he would do next. He, too, could feel the danger even as he longingly watched the man drive away.

•

He felt a wrenching pain in his gut as he opened his eyes and tried to focus. His mouth and throat were parched. They were so parched, in fact, that he could barely swallow his own saliva. There was a steady pounding in his head and an irregular beating in his temples.

For a brief moment, he didn't know who he was. *What is my name? What the hell is my name? Francis. No, that's not it. I hate that name. Frank? Is it Frank? Okay, I know it's Frank.*

The sound in his ears wasn't quite a ringing sound so much as it was a continuous buzzing that reverberated from his ears into his entire body. He speculated if the weird buzzing was the morning after feeling from the side effects of way too much bourbon. In all his years, he'd never felt like this before, but there was always a first time. *Maybe I had a stroke. I've heard of that happening to young guys ... no, probably not.*

As groggy and weak as he was, all of these thoughts went through his mind immediately as he struggled to regain full consciousness. *Come on, Frank. Snap out of it.*

He raised himself slowly and painfully into a sitting position, leaning his back gingerly against a rough stone wall. He tried to flex his muscles and joints, attempting to work out the intense sensations that coursed throughout his body. He could feel the cold of the rough stone behind him and it chilled and pained his back. But, at the same time, he felt waves of uncomfortable heat coursing through his body. Cold, clammy and feverishly hot, all blending together inside him.

As he examined his surroundings in the dim light, he saw that the room around him appeared to consist of dank concrete walls. He could feel the damp and somewhat slimy concrete on his back as he leaned against the wall.

He sensed, rather than saw, insects crawling across the walls and across his body. He shivered in loathing at the idea that spiders and roaches and all of the other basement vermin were dancing on his flesh. He desperately tried to slap and scratch them off his body, but he realized his muscles wouldn't cooperate. Just one smack exhausted him. *Why am I so tired?*

The flooring that he sat on appeared to be hard packed dirt. *I'm sitting in dirt.* The floor, like the walls, was cold and unforgiving. He heard tiny scratching noises all around him on the floor. *What the hell is that?* Involuntarily, he whimpered in fear. *Stay off me, you little bastards. Get the hell off me. Get off.*

Above him, there was a solitary low-watt lightbulb dangling from the ceiling. The air in the room smelled just like an old moldy cellar should smell. He believed he was in an empty basement, someone's basement. *But who's basement am I in ... and why?*

With an almost inaudible rasp, he muttered, "Where in the hell am I?" as he strained to shift his body. "How did I get here?"

He realized that his shirt and shoes were missing. He was barefoot. He could feel every part of his body quivering from the cold that surrounded him. Heat coursed through his body in unnatural and uncomfortable waves, almost like erratic heart beats. The whole setting was alarmingly perplexing to him.

His brain was fuzzy and muddled and his memories weren't coming to the surface. *I know I'm Frank, but what else ... what else is there?* He tried to recall what had occurred and what brought him to this basement.

Shivering, he closed his eyes and tried to recount recent events, or any event that might help him. It was then that he realized no memories were making their way out. He didn't even know how long he'd been down in this dirt room. *Why can't I think straight?*

As his eyes got more accustomed to the dim light, he noticed that across the basement there was a flight of wooden stairs that led to a door at the top. Even though his tongue felt like sandpaper and his voice was raspy, he tried to suppress his mounting hysteria and calmly called out, "Hello up there. Can anyone hear me?"

He heard no response. He coughed and tried to clear his throat.

He tried it again. "Hello? Is there anyone up there that can help me?"

Again, there was no response. There was only an unnerving stillness. The main thing that he could sense was an eerie and uncomfortable stirring silence. Silence that was deafening and terrifying. *Don't forget the creepy-crawlers, Frank. I know they're here.*

In his present condition, he wasn't sure if he could make it to the stairs. He tried to stand up, but only got as far as the kneeling position before he realized he was far too weak to get all the way to his feet. He collapsed back down to the floor and let out a deep groan. The twisting pain in his gut was overpowering.

Already exhausted from only a minimal amount of movement, he laid face down on the dirt floor and fought the overwhelming urge to drift back into sleep again. He didn't know how many times he had drifted between sleep and wakefulness. Fighting to stay alert, he rolled over onto his back and laid there, trying to evoke any tiny memory that could help him make sense of his current situation. *I have to figure this out because there's nobody here to do it for me. I can do this. I just have to close my eyes and concentrate.*

Finally, after more than an hour of intense concentration, he remembered the last place he'd been before waking up in the basement. *I was in a lounge. No, it wasn't a lounge. It was some seedy dive bar called The Twisted Tail.*

He laid there, on the dirt, shivering from the chill that came from the relentless dampness all around him. Then another significant piece of the puzzle slid into place. *And there was an old jukebox in the corner playing song after song. Yes, I can remember the old jukebox. I met a woman there, a beautiful woman. Yes, that's it. I met a woman and I bought her a drink. It's getting clearer. After that, we got up and slow danced next to the pool table for a little while.*

Memories of her appearance and presence came flooding in like a tidal wave. He could see her as if she was standing right there in front of him. *She had dark red, shoulder-length hair and striking green eyes. Her teeth and her smile were perfect.* He recalled that she was tall and thin but still quite shapely. And her fragrance had been powdery and slightly spicy.

As he was still trying to fight his stupor, he even recalled that she was wearing a tight white top and a pair of jeans that revealed every curve from the waist down. *She had silver hoop earrings and rings, lots of rings on her fingers ... maybe she had them on all ten fingers.* He remembered noticing a silver chain with an unusual charm or amulet which hung around her slender neck.

His mind went to the night at the bar when he'd met the redhead and bought her the drink after they'd made lingering eye contact with each other. Actually, he remembered now, that other than the bartender, they'd been the only two people in the bar. *Not so hard to buy the girl a drink.* He shook his head wryly.

He recalled that, in spite of their mutual attraction, they hadn't had much to say to each other, at least, nothing substantial. He recalled that her name was … *Karen. Yes, that was it. Now it's all starting to come back to me. The woman's name was Karen.*

•

"Karen, that's a beautiful name." *Was that a lame pickup line or what? Maybe I should've just asked what her sign was, or said, here I am, what are your other two wishes.* "Hello, Karen. My name is Frank."

Frank asked the bartender to get the woman another drink. He noticed she had been sipping on a dirty vodka martini, straight up with two olives. He had his usual bourbon on the rocks with a splash of ginger ale and a couple of cocktail onions laid on top. He laid some cash down on the bar while he listened to the music playing on the jukebox. It was some early 70's song, before his time, but nice and romantic.

As Frank swung around on his barstool and looked into Karen's eyes, he tapped his fingers on the bar to the beat of the song and asked, "Would you like to dance? This is a good song."

The tiny bar had no real dancefloor but they managed to find a spot near the pool tables. Instead of actually dancing, the two of them basically stood there, pressed up against each other, swaying to the slow music, and staring deeply into each other's eyes. Frank sang, or at least tried to sing along with the song under his breath. "Don't let me be lonely tonight …"

Karen smiled at him and went along with his slightly tone-deaf serenade, thinking he was sweetly more attractive for it.

When the song had finished, they sauntered back to the bar to finish their drinks. Frank had high hopes of how the rest of the night would play out. *I hope I'm going to score tonight!*

It had been quite a dry spell for him lately. Karen asked, "Do you live in these parts, Frank? I don't think I've ever seen you here at The Twisted Tail. This is such a small town. I usually know most of the faces in here."

He explained, "No, I don't live here. I was just passing through, got tired and got a room at the motel across the street." He was careful not to bring up the incident that happened on the dark road just outside of town.

Frank was taller than average and had a slender, muscular build. As busy as his life was, he still made time for regular workouts at the gym. He had dark shaggy hair, blue eyes and ruddy skin. His features were more strong than perfect, which suited him just fine. He exuded masculine confidence and a roguish charisma that drew people into his orbit. Women often gave him the "second look." That's what Karen was doing now, giving him the look. He enjoyed the attention.

Seductively, she ran the tip of her middle finger around the rim of her martini glass. Then she flirtatiously ran her finger across her lips to taste the vodka. She was curious. "So, are you on vacation or something?"

"God, no. I only wish that I was on vacation. I can't remember the last time I had a vacation. No, I'm driving from Harrisburg down to Baton Rouge on a business trip."

"What kind of business?"

"Sales."

"Sales? That's interesting." Karen actually didn't find sales interesting but she wanted to find a way to continue the conversation.

Frank shrugged his shoulders. "Well, it's probably not interesting to the average person, but I like it and it pays the bills."

"Harrisburg to Baton Rouge? Wow, that is quite a drive."

"Tell me about it. When I felt myself getting too tired behind the wheel, I stopped here and got a room right there across the street at the Collinsville Motel." He realized that was the second time he'd mentioned the motel room to her. *Don't blow this, Frank. It's been way too long.*

She smiled and then giggled as she took another long sip of her martini. Then, she ate the olives slowly and seductively. After consuming another drink, Frank took a lasting gulp of his bourbon and ginger, set the glass down on the bar and whispered to Karen, "Would you excuse me for a minute?"

She asked, "Where are you going?"

Frank chuckled, leaned in and whispered, "Nature calls. I'll be right back." He made his way to the men's room.

Frank stood at the urinal and pondered how the rest of the night would go. *I think that tonight might be the night. One more drink and I can get her to come back to the motel with me. And she's hot, best I've seen in a long time.*

Only a few minutes later, Frank came out of the men's room and walked back to the bar but

Karen was gone. He saw his rocks glass still sitting on the bar but her martini glass was gone. As he glanced around the room, he asked the bartender, "Excuse me. The woman that I was just talking to. Do you know where she went?"

The well-built attractive bartender shook his head when he replied, "I don't know which woman you're talking about, mister."

Frank knew the bartender had to know who he was talking about since they were the only two customers there. "The woman. The same woman I was standing here with. Her name was Karen." *Is this guy blind?*

"There's a lot of women that come in and out of here every night, mister. I can't keep an eye on all of them."

Frank glanced around the room again and saw that there was no one else there. He was getting angry at the bartender's nonchalant attitude. *This guy must think he's being some kind of a comedian.* Frank's voice got louder. "The redhead that was drinking the dirty vodka martinis with me. She was the only other person that was in here. How could you not see her?"

The thirty-five-year-old bartender, whose name tag told the business traveler that his name was Eddie, shrugged his shoulders and continued to polish the rims of his freshly washed bar glasses. He continued to appear puzzled. "I don't know, mister. I've been kind of busy back here."

Frank's voice was becoming aggressive and he was using a lot of hand gestures as he explained, "The woman! The redhead I've been standing with and dancing with since I got here. For Christ's sake, Eddie, she was standing right here in front of you and drinking dirty martinis."

"No, sir. I don't know where she went … if she was even here at all. I don't remember seeing you at the bar with any redhead." He looked down at Frank's glass, chuckled and asked, "Don't you think that maybe you've had enough to drink for one night? That's your third one, mister." *Now the asshole is saying I'm drunk!*

"You know exactly how many drinks I've had but you can't remember seeing a woman that was standing right in front of you?" Again, Eddie shrugged his shoulders.

Upset with the bartender's ignorance and attitude, he hurriedly drank the rest of his bourbon, slammed the glass on the bar and shouted, "Thanks for nothing, buddy!"

In a fit of rage, Frank stormed out of the bar and decided he should probably return to the motel. He was tired of asking the bartender where Karen had disappeared to. *What kind of racket were they running anyway?* He felt like a fool and an idiot. *Damned motherfuckers!*

Besides, he knew he had to get back on the interstate to Baton Rouge first thing in the morning and he shouldn't waste his time trying to figure out why Karen skipped out on him. *Yessiree, his night of fun was over. Guess the dry spell hasn't ended ... motherfuckers.*

As the cool outside air hit him in the face, he began to walk slower and even stagger a little. He had never had a few glasses of bourbon hit him that quickly. Vaguely, he muttered to himself, "I should have eaten something for dinner."

As he was about to cross the street, he began to feel extremely dizzy, lightheaded and sick to his stomach. He looked up and everything started to spin around as he fell down onto his knees. He felt a devastating weakening in his stomach. It was a slow churning that was getting more and more intense by the second. He faced the ground when he thought he was going to vomit.

Each time he tried to look up, everything was swaying in his head, like having vertigo. Then, Frank saw Eddie, the bartender, standing only a few feet away from him. *Where in the hell did this prick come from?*

Eddie asked, "Hey, are you okay, mister? I noticed that you were stumbling out the front door and I came out to see if I could do anything to help." *Go to hell, Eddie.*

In a quiet but sarcastic tone, Frank laughed and responded, "No. I'm not okay, Eddie. I'm on my knees in the middle of some nowhere town and about to bring up the greasy cheeseburger omelet that I ate for breakfast. Does it look like I'm okay, Eddie? Does it look like I'm okay?"

Eddie leaned down and remarked, "Geez man, you don't have to be such an asshole," before he put his arms around Frank's chest and lifted him back onto his feet. Then, he put Frank's arm around his shoulder and started walking him slowly back towards the bar.

Frank, with very little strength left, tried to stop Eddie as he protested, "I don't want to go back to that damned bar! I don't want to go this way, you idiot! I'm going to the motel!"

"I'm just trying to help and you're looking a little green right now."

Frank tried to drag his feet; in fact, he could barely walk now, but Eddie had enough strength to carry him the rest of the way. Frustrated because he was being overpowered by the bartender, he yelled, "Fuck you, Eddie!"

"That's not a very nice thing to say, mister. You shouldn't curse at people that are trying to give you a hand."

"I just told you that we're going the wrong way. I need to get back to my motel room across the street! Damn you!"

"We're just going in for a minute and then I'll take you back to the motel."

Angrily, Frank continued. "I have to be on the road early in the morning! Take me back to the motel now!" Eddie ignored his demands and took him back into the bar.

Once they were inside, Frank noticed that all of the lights were turned off except for the red one that dangled over the pool table. The old jukebox was unplugged and not lit up anymore. Frank tried to stop Eddie by pounding his hands on Eddie's back but even his hands didn't seem to have much strength at that point.

Eddie helped prop Frank up, in his declining state, on a barstool, then just left him there with his back leaning up against the bar. Frank tried his best to stay upright.

Without another word, Eddie walked into the back room while Frank struggled there, feeling lightheaded, queasy and frail. He could hear Eddie moving around in the backroom. He tried to shout, "Hey! I need help in here!" but his words weren't coming out the way he wanted them too. They were too low for Eddie to hear.

With his head hung down, he tried to shout out to the bartender again. "I need to get back to the motel, Eddie! I'm on a very tight schedule, you little asshole! I have to be back on the road first thing in the morning!" Aside from "you little asshole," his words were unintelligible. He felt his body getting weaker.

He heard no response from that damned idiot. After he waited a few more minutes, he could feel himself gradually slipping off the barstool and falling onto the floor. He looked up at the bar one more time and wanted to call out to Eddie for help but couldn't seem to muster the words. That was the last thing Frank remembered before he woke up in the basement.

●

Marjorie answered the phone call and was standing with her phone up to her ear. "What do you mean he didn't show up for the sales meeting in Baton Rouge? I talked to him when he was driving out of Harrisburg. I don't know what could have happened." Marjorie should have sounded more worried than she was, recalling the several times Frank just decided to steer the car in the direction of Vegas.

"I haven't heard a word from him since. Yes, I'd tell you if I had."

Marjorie was becoming angry at the fact that Frank's boss was implying she might be lying. She was also irritated that Frank might be back up to his old tricks. It wasn't the first time and probably not the last.

"No, I don't know what a big deal this sales meeting was. I told you once and I'm not going to tell you again. I don't know where my brother is and I haven't heard from him."

She was stunned. "Hold on a minute! You're firing him because he missed one goddam business meeting in goddam Baton Rouge?"

Then, Marjorie placed her free hand on her forehead. She knew a headache was building. "But why would you do that? After all, Frank's the best salesman you have and the only salesman you have that's stupid enough to drive all the way around the country for you!"

Marjorie heard her children arguing in the next room. "Listen, I have a family to take care of and I don't think I want to hear anymore from you tonight. Goodbye!"

She slammed the phone down in the cradle and put both hands on her forehead. She said under her breath, "You better have a good reason for this one, Frank."

Marjorie was furious that Frank was most likely in some strip club in Sin City and not lying in a ditch alongside some desolate highway. "And he just lost the best job he ever had."

The children were still in the living room quarreling with each over who was in control of the television remote. Marjorie turned and marched into the room, took the remote from Benny's hand and, directing her anger at Frank towards them, asserted, "No one gets the remote!"

Benny crossed his arms, kicked his legs and pouted before he cried out, "But mom, she started it!" He was on the verge of a tantrum which made Marjorie angrier.

"I don't care who started it! I'm sure that you both have homework to finish! Go upstairs and finish it!"

The children, both pouting, knew that their mother meant business. They knew that certain look in her eyes that told them to do what she said or dad would handle it later.

•

Frank lifted his head and smelled the foul odor of mold, not knowing how long he'd been asleep this time.

The cold and dank basement still looked as it had before. He was completely alone. He didn't know if anyone else had been there when he was sleeping.

He tried to remember what had happened to him after Eddie carelessly propped him up on that barstool. And he wondered again where Karen had gone. *Karen was such a good-looking woman. We could have had something together, at least for one night. I wish I knew why she left like that. I thought we were connecting.* He knew that Eddie must have seen her while they were standing at the bar and when she ducked out. None of it made any sense to Frank, but right now he was too scared and worried to be angry.

As he rolled over onto his side, still feeling a gut-wrenching pain in his stomach, he could see a steady light beaming from below the door at the top of the stairs. He strained to call out, "Hello, can you hear me?"

There was only silence.

His throat hurt with every word. "Eddie! Are you up there?"

There was no response.

Trying to call out exhausted him. "Eddie, can you hear me?"

Nothing.

He begged for some kind of response. "If you can hear me, come down here and help me. I think I need a doctor."

Frank knew before he even opened his mouth again that there would be no response to his frequent pleas for help.

For several minutes, he attempted to crawl on his belly towards the stairs but, once again, his fragile state only allowed him to move a few inches closer to his goal. *What the hell is wrong with me? Why am I so weak?*

The struggle to move caused even more pain in his stomach. A wave of exhaustion rushed over him again as the pain became overwhelming. Frank laid his head on the dirt floor, trying to suppress his moans of agony. *At least the damned spiders don't scare me anymore.* He stared up at the light before his eyes grew so heavy that he could no longer keep them open.

•

In a moment of unexpected surprise, Frank quickly opened his eyes when he felt that hard-packed dirt floor beginning to give way underneath him. *What the hell is this? It isn't possible. It's collapsing!*

He was dropping lower and lower and he tried to claw his way back onto the solid dirt. *I have to fight this!*

Nothing helped and Frank found himself slipping through the floor and plummeting into a hollow and profound darkness. He continued to fall deeper and deeper into what seemed to be a cavern, a bottomless cavern. *Oh my God, what is this?*

He opened his eyes and saw nothing but blackness all around him as he bounced off the sides of the tunnel, feeling every jab, scrape and laceration that the jagged rock walls inflicted on his already aching body. *I'm going to die. I'm going to die.*

He looked down and, in stark contrast to the unnerving blackness, he saw red, orange and blue flames leaping and reaching towards him, beckoning him to join them. Although the flames seemed several miles below him, he could hear them crackling and laughing in anticipation of burning him alive. *What the hell is this?*

He screamed out for help but there was no one there to help him. He could feel himself dropping at an ever-accelerating rate towards the bottom of the tunnel. He knew that when he reached bottom, he would surely die. He cried out again, but there was no response. *What did I do to deserve this?*

Unexpectedly, he could hear a muffled whispering as he dropped ever faster. The whispers sounded almost like laughter. "Help me! Someone, help me!" The quiet whispers continued to laugh and taunt him. *Where is that coming from?*

Frank looked down again and saw that he was getting closer to the flames that continued to spit and crackle riotously. He closed his eyes and the faint laughter stopped abruptly.

He knew that he had only seconds before he would hit bottom and die. He wondered why his life wasn't passing before his eyes, but then again, he didn't want to die. He didn't want to feel the excruciating pain of dying. He screamed out one more time, "Please! Help me! Someone, help me!"

•

When Frank opened his eyes, his hands were trembling and his forehead was dripping with beads of sweat.

He glanced around at his surroundings and was actually relieved to see that he was in the same dank basement, lying on the same unfriendly hard-packed dirt floor. He felt a chill down his spine when he noticed that he had been moved back to his original position in the large room.

What a freakin' nightmare. It all felt so real. As sluggish as he was, his mind careened between random thoughts of what was happening to him. *What kind of drugs did they give me? Did they rufy me? Date rape drugs? Nah ... I'd feel better than I do now. I hope my face isn't messed up. The ladies won't like that. That lousy bartender. Everything started with him. He'll never make another drink for me. I can tell you ...*

He contemplated his next move. *But what is my next move if I'm not even capable of moving? I have to think. I have to think.* Suddenly, he could hear someone walking around directly above his head. Frank tried to sit up as best he could. His voice was still hoarse but he tried to cry out for help yet again. "Someone, please help me. Is anyone up there?"

The footsteps stopped abruptly. There was no response.

"Eddie! I know you're up there."

Still nothing. The footsteps started walking around again.

"Please get me out of here. What am I doing down here?"

Whoever was walking in the room above his head stopped again. Frank lifted his head and gazed up towards the ceiling and waited.

"I know you can hear me. Just let me go and I'll never say anything to anyone about this. I'll just walk away."

There was a brief moment of stillness before he heard the footsteps above his head begin again. He could tell, by the heavy sound of the steps that the person above him was a man.

Frank noticed that the pain in his gut was still present but not quite as severe as it had been before. He still felt unbelievably weak and was beginning to feel something akin to hunger. As his pain was beginning to subside, his anger reemerged. He was worn-out from being the victim in whatever game was being played, and he knew Eddie had some involvement in the game. Victimhood did not suit him.

He looked across the room and knew he had to keep trying. *I know he's up there. I know it was that damned bartender, Eddie.* That's when Frank decided to make another move towards the wooden stairs. He rolled back over and attempted to crawl on his belly again.

He saw, from where he was positioned, that there was no light at the top of the stairs anymore and no footsteps echoed in the room over his head. Still, he moved painfully forward, using his filthy aching elbows to help push him through the dirt on his belly in a swimming motion. Back and forth. Back and forth. *I can do this.*

This time Frank made it several feet in thirty minutes. He could see that the bottom step was only ten feet away. He felt encouraged to make it the rest of the way but his weakened body wouldn't let him continue. *No! Don't give up on me now. It's just a little further.*

Suddenly, he heard a whimper. He couldn't tell if it was a man's or a woman's voice that made the noise. Was this just another nightmare or was it real? He didn't know. *I wish I could tell between what's real and not real. I have to keep a clear head and focus.*

His efforts to crawl across the dirt floor had exhausted him so completely that he couldn't even try to respond to yet another weak groan coming from somewhere in the basement. He was tired, so tired. He laid his head down in the dirt and lost consciousness again.

•

Frank found himself walking across a room, a dark and rather musty room. He noticed that all of his pain was gone but he was still shirtless and shoeless. He saw that all of the furnishings and the room structure were not of modern times. It appeared as if he was in an old castle.

The room was large and had soaring ceilings with colorful paintings interspersed with gold leaf. Candles, smelling of beeswax that almost masked a slightly fetid odor, flickered in the filtered darkness. The room was superbly furnished, in contrast to the lingering foul smell. *This is one of those screwed up dreams. It has to be.*

Frank skulked slowly and quietly down an extensive and carpeted corridor, into a ballroom where he saw couples dancing by candlelight. He knew nothing about dance, and not too much about this period in history, but, for some odd reason, he knew that they were dancing the Allemande.

The assembly of musicians played music that he recognized as the baroque style from the mid-seventeenth century. *Why do I know that? How can I know that? Did I read it somewhere?* He observed, curious, but no one noticed him standing there.

He cautiously stepped closer to the dancing couples until one of the women, who was dressed in a golden yellow gown with a winged collar, glanced away from the dancing and saw Frank, bare chested and filthy. She pointed at him and screamed.

The musicians ended their song abruptly. The well-dressed men turned and began staring at Frank while the curious women backed away from him.

A tall bearded man with long curly salt and pepper hair, wearing an orange-colored doublet with wide wings and fitted sleeves, approached Frank cautiously. He asked, "Are you lost?"

"No. I don't think so."

The man, taller than Frank, stared down at him and snobbishly questioned, "Are you a servant of the king's palace? Do you work in the kitchen?"

Frank shook his head. "No, I know I'm not one of the servants."

Suspiciously, the bearded man inquired, "Do you even belong here?"

"No, I don't think I do."

The man's voice got loud as his face turned red from anger. "Then, why are you here where you were not invited?"

Frank bowed his head. "I wish I knew. I don't know how I got here."

The man stared at Frank's bare chest and his dirty bare feet. "And you are half naked in the king's house. Just where is your blouse and shoes?"

Frank was getting angry and frustrated because he knew that he couldn't answer the man's inquiries. "I don't know. I don't know. I wish I did but I don't."

The tall man was losing his patience with Frank's answers. "Then, if you are not one of the king's servants and you have not been invited, why in the hell are you here?" The tall man let out an arrogant chuckle.

"I told you. I don't know."

The man waved his hand in the air so all could see. "This is a private event in honor of the lady of the castle and you are not an invited guest. I think it is time for you to leave. Someone will show you the way out."

"I think this is a dream."

The man smiled condescendingly. "You think this is a dream?"

"Yes." Frank nodded.

The man continued, making fun of Frank. "So, we are all supposed to believe that we are just part of your dream?"

Frank bowed his head and replied, "Yes. I think that you are part of it." *It isn't real. None of the people are real.*

The tall man turned back and smiled at everyone else in the room. They began to chuckle at Frank. Then, the chuckle turned into a loud roar of laughter. "I think it is time for you to wake up so we can all disappear. If not, then get out of here."

"I want to wake up. Believe me. I want to wake up."

Suddenly, a dark shadow, an ashen haze passed through the room and then vanished in a flash.

One of the women in the room screamed and then fell to the ballroom floor. She laid there on her back. Then another woman dropped and then one of the men did the same.

Soon, everyone in the room, musicians and dancers alike, was lying on the floor. The tall man with the salt and pepper hair was the last person to drop onto his back. Everyone squirmed around the black and white checkered dancefloor and moaned in agonizing pain. Most stared up at Frank.

Almost imperceptibly, the atmosphere changed. A gradual darkening began to take over the room. Frank blinked his eyes rapidly trying to clear his vision.

Then, a translucent red fog emerged from out of nowhere, seeming to cloak everyone and everything in a murky crimson shroud. More of the people on the floor moaned in agony. *Why is this happening?*

He heard one woman scream, as she pointed up at Frank, "He is a monster. He is a creature of the night!" Then, one after another, they seemed to diminish into slack-jawed, open eyed stillness. *Why are they like this? Why didn't it affect me? Why am I alright and all of them are dead?*

Frank remained standing there in shock as he watched the spectacle. His hands were trembling and his breaths were rapid. He felt the droplets of hot sweat as they trickled down from his forehead.

With mounting alarm, he pivoted jerkily around the room, staring into all of the lifeless eyes, looking for any kind of explanation for the events that had unfolded before him. Escape was his primary objective. *I've got to get out of here! I've got to get out! I've got to wake up from this nightmare!*

•

Frank jerked and opened his eyes as he gradually returned to consciousness. Once again, he found himself lying face down in the cold dirt. The discomfort in his stomach was back and it was more intense than before.

The pain made it feel as if his stomach had been torn open. He groaned in anguish as he rolled his body around onto his back and lifted his head. He didn't think he could feel any worse than before, but he did. *I feel like I'm going to die.* Each time he moved slightly in any direction, he believed he was going to heave.

He noticed that there was no sound coming from the room above his head. He waited and tried to pick up on any little noise. Nothing. It was quiet. There were no heavy footsteps up there. Nothing but ominous silence.

Frank wanted to maneuver his body towards the staircase again but, along with the renewed pain, he felt weaker than he had before. He tried to push himself into an upright position but he was able to get only halfway up before his stomach began to twist and churn again.

Frank wondered if he was going to die all alone in that goddam basement. Not a man to give up, however, he pushed that idea aside and began looking for another reason for his dire situation. *I must have been drugged by someone. That's the only explanation it could be. But now that I'm here, what do they want from me? I know it was that goddam bartender. I know it.*

He laid back down on the dirt floor and tried to conserve his energy this time. Just then, he heard that faint moan coming from somewhere in the huge damp cellar. He whispered, "Is there someone else in here?"

The sad whimpering went on for a few more seconds before he said, "Just tell me where you are. Maybe I can help you."

A barely intelligible voice muttered, "I'm over here. I'm over here."

It was a woman's voice. *Oh my God, I'm not alone down here.* Frank rolled on his side and tried to look around the room for some type of movement or a shadow but there was none. "I can't tell where you are. Help me out. Can you move around to give me a sign?"

She gasped in pain and then said, "I can't move at all."

"Are you injured?"

"I'm exhausted and I'm very weak. I can't stay awake anymore."

Nervously, Frank said, "Please, don't go back to sleep. I won't be able to find where you are if I can't hear you." *You can't go back to sleep. We have to figure this out together.*

"I'm sorry. I can't keep my eyes open. I'm so sorry."

He didn't hear her voice again. He realized she must have been just as hurt and tired as he was. He tried to push himself forward to the middle of the basement floor to see if he could find her but, after a few slight moves and a few sharp twists to his stomach, Frank found himself fighting the pain in his gut and the intense physical exhaustion. *This isn't working.*

Then, he heard the same heavy footsteps walking around in the room above his head. He stared up at the ceiling but remained silent. *Why does he want me? I'm nobody important. I can't be held for ransom. Everybody in my life is basically broke.*

He didn't even try to call out to the person who was upstairs. Instead, he laid his head back down and fell asleep.

•

Frank stood there, in the center of the hazy room where all the people around him were dressed in pinstriped suits or provocative little dresses, and everyone had a drink in their hand.

There were several women on a small stage dancing to the wild and exciting jazz music. The musicians, sitting off to the side, played a piano, a bass and several different horns.

Frank looked around and realized he was in a speakeasy. He thought it must be the 1920's when the period of prohibition was at its peak and the dangerous world of bootleggers and mobsters was in full swing. *Why am I here? Why am I dreaming about all these places I never thought about before?*

The free-spirited women had bobbed hair and red lips. They arched their backs and flirted in their sleek and Avant Garde flapper dresses. These were the modern women of the late 1920's.

They were rebellious, deliberate, focused and robust.

The men swaggered and touched their slicked-back hair, whispering sweet nothings and indecent proposals to the women, and trading lewd jokes with the other men. It was a new world for them.

As the jazz music continued to play, all of them threw back their heads and laughed in frenzied enjoyment of life and the forbidden elixirs that were banned by the noble experiment of prohibition. They didn't care.

Electricity was available, because there was one naked lightbulb hanging from the low ceiling, and one anemic fan blowing the stale air that was filled with thick clouds of evil smelling cigar and cigarette smoke.

Otherwise, the ambience was completed with a few oil lamps and a blacked-out window, set high on a low wall. *Frank looked around the speakeasy and realized where he was. Oh God, help me. Not another basement.*

Frank wasn't noticed by anyone at first until one of the rough thugs turned, gave him a shifty look and pointed at him, shouting, "Hey! What the hella you doin' in here? How did ya get in here?"

Frank looked down and saw that he was shirtless and shoeless again, and still filthy from lying on a dirt floor. "I don't know how I got here, wherever here is."

The tough guy didn't waste a moment as he called out to two of his henchmen. "Jimmy! Sonny! I smell a rat. Get over here and get dis guy outta here ... now!"

The music stopped immediately when two enormous guys in gray suits came out from behind the bar and steamrolled their big bodies aggressively towards Frank. Sonny said, "I bet he's workin' for da Lombardo or the Rizzo families."

They grabbed him by the upper arms and began to drag him out. Frank was so caught up in the action of the room, he hardly had time to react to the two henchmen. "No please, I'm not working for anybody. I think that you are part of my dream."

Jimmy laughed like a bulldog. "Hey boss, he thinks he's just dreamin' us!"

The boss, with half a cigar in the corner of his mouth, slapped his hand down on a table and laughed out loud. Everyone else followed suit and stared to laugh.

Just then, a dark shadow passed over the room slowly. People began to drop to the floor as they had in his last dream. Bottles of whiskey began to burst open on their own. Glasses slid off the tables and bar and shattered everywhere. Jimmy and Sonny let go of Frank as they began to feel weak too. Again, everything in the room was tinted a murky red.

The last person to drop onto the floor was Sonny. As he lay there, he looked up and asked, "What the hell did ya do to me? You're a monster. Nothin' but a fuckin' monster. You'll pay for this."

Frank watched in sheer horror as all the people wriggled around like earthworms on the floor, struggling to breathe, until they were still. They were dead.

Frank gasped as he gazed around at the old 1920's speakeasy, the broken glass on the floor, the red hue of the room, and the forty-odd dead people lying on the floor and up on the stage.

He stepped on the broken glass with his bare feet but didn't feel the shards cutting into his skin. There was no blood and no pain. He walked to the door of the speakeasy and was just about to open it, hoping freedom would be on the other side.

He heard a faint and haunting echo waft across the room. The echo sounded like the laughter he'd heard when he was falling into hell. *Oh, dear God, it's like the goddam angel of death came through here, like in the castle, like in the Bible.*

•

A loud slamming noise and heavy footsteps woke Frank up this time. He lifted his head and saw the shadow of a dark figure walking through the basement. He didn't know if he was actually awake or if this was still part of his crazy dream. He shook his head to make sure he was awake.

Once he realized that the dream was over, he attempted to call out but his mouth was parched and his tongue was extremely dry. He could only mutter for help in a soft voice. "I don't know who you are, but please, I'm here."

The shadowy figure disappeared from view while Frank tried again. "Can you please help me? I'm injured and weak."

Frank heard a noise that came from a corner of the basement that he couldn't see. The noise was a bold thud, like someone was being thrown down on the dirt floor. "Hey, can you hear me? I'm right over here."

Frank heard the sound of a door opening and closing and then there was complete stillness again. This told Frank that there must be a door to freedom nearby on the other side of the room. He realized he wouldn't have to climb that wooden staircase to get freed.

He suddenly felt an adrenaline rush as he rolled over on his belly and began to push himself forward again. He made it only three feet across the room before the pain became so excruciating that he had to stop.

Frank put his head down and took time to think about his next move. *How the hell can I get all the way across the basement when I can't even move a couple feet?*

Several minutes later, he again heard the same woman moaning. With a desperate plea, he whispered, "I'm here. Can you hear me? I'm right over here."

Suddenly, the moaning became a woman's voice. Trying to speak loud enough for Frank to hear, she said, "I'm over here. I'm in the dark and I can't see you."

"Can you walk to me?"

"No. I'm not strong enough."

"Can you walk at all?"

"I already tried but I can't even get off the ground. I'm feeling a whole lot of discomfort and I can hardly move."

Just then, a light went off in Frank's head when he recognized the voice. "Are you the same girl that I met at the bar?"

"The same girl? When?"

"Is your name Karen?"

She whispered, "Is it you?

Knowing it was Karen, some hope crept into his voice. He answered, "Yes. It's me. I'm the guy from the bar."

"Frank?"

"Yes, It's Frank."

She grunted and groaned before she asked, "What happened to us?"

"I'm not sure but I think it was Eddie, that bartender, who did this."

"Eddie? Why would he do this?"

Frank didn't want to get into why he thought Eddie was responsible. He wanted to figure out the rest of the night. "Karen, what's the last thing you can remember?"

"I remember you going into the men's room at the bar. As soon as you left, I remember taking another sip of my martini and waiting. Then … it felt like someone hit me over the back of the head. I must have blacked out."

It was then that Karen grasped too that the bartender must have been the one. "It had to have been Eddie. That bastard. He was the only other one in the bar."

Frank rolled over on his side in an attempt to find comfort. "I came back from the bathroom and Eddie had already cleaned up your drink. Then, he said he never saw me with a woman that night. He acted as if you were never even there. For a minute, I thought I was going crazy."

He could hear Karen struggling to find a comfortable position too. She grunted a few times before she asked, "What the hell are we doing here, Frank? And where is here anyway?"

Frank lifted himself up on one elbow. "I think we're in the cellar beneath the bar. It has to be Eddie that did this to us."

"Why is he doing this?"

"I don't know why." Frank began to feel that penetrating pain in his gut again. He rolled back over onto his back and said, "When I just woke up, I heard a loud noise on your side of the room and then I saw someone's shadow. Did you see anything over there?"

"No," Karen replied. "I must have still been unconscious."

"Look around, do you see anything different that wasn't there before?"

There were a few minutes of silence. Frank knew that Karen was struggling to find something that had changed. She finally managed to get the words out. "It's so dark over here, Frank. I can't tell what's around me. I can barely see what's a couple feet in front of me."

Frank was sure of what he heard. "I know I heard a door open and close over there. Can you see a door?"

Suddenly, her breathing got shallow and rapid. She let out a sigh of pain. "I told you that I can't see anything over here. I don't feel so good. I think I'm going to pass out."

"No, Karen, you have to fight the fatigue. If we don't fight, we'll never discover a way to get out of here."

Frank waited for her to say, "Okay, Frank. I'm wide awake." But she didn't say it.

He rolled onto his side and waited to hear something but she didn't say anything. He called out to her. "Karen. Karen. Are you there?" She didn't respond.

It wasn't long before Frank's eyelids were growing heavy too. *Oh shit! I'm going to fall asleep again.*

He tried to fight it but he was fighting a losing battle. He laid his head down on the dirt and fell asleep again.

•

Frank opened his eyes slowly. He found himself standing in the middle of a magnificent garden. The garden was filled with vibrant trees, beautiful flowers, colorful birds, and animals of many varieties.

The colors of the grass, trees and sky were intense and breathtaking. Never in his life had he seen such vivid colors. The fragrance of the flowers was so sublime that Frank became giddy and light headed. All of the animals were healthy, sleek and in their prime.

He noticed that the beasts in the garden were all mingling freely and peacefully with each other. Several of the young animals of different species were scampering playfully around each other.

Frank knew that panthers, sheep, bears and hyenas didn't coexist peacefully in the real world. *This isn't how animals should act. After all, there's a food chain and many of these creatures are on the bottom.* Be that as it may, those animals who were natural enemies seemed not to know or care how nature had designed them.

He walked carefully through the garden, through the peaceful animals, and through the fragrant flowers, until he heard the sound of voices. He stopped and hid behind a big tree to listen. He peered around the tree to see who was speaking. He saw a lovely naked woman with long chestnut-brown hair leaning back against a tall persimmon tree.

He saw there was a long gray, snakelike creature with tiny useless legs that was hanging from one of the branches. Frank gasped when he heard the snake speaking to the woman in a low seductive voice. "I see that you're alone, my lovely one. Where is your man? Is he neglecting you again?"

The young woman responded in a soft and hesitant voice. "He has left the garden. He will be gone for a while."

"Why has he left the garden?"

"To walk. To gather. To think. He is the man. That is what he does."

The snake suppressed his flare of resentment towards the man and said, "Then, there is time for us to pursue the great pleasure together as we have discussed. There is no one here to stop us."

The young woman said, "You discussed it, sir. I only listened. I do not believe this thing should be done. My father would not want me to stray from Adam."

Frank let out a long breath when he realized where he was. *Hold on a minute. Adam, a garden, and a snake. That must be Eve. What the hell?*

The deceitful snake slithered down the tree a little closer to Eve as he continued the conversation. "But, my dear sweet Eve, you have misunderstood what your father meant. Yes, perhaps he did say that you are not to partake of the forbidden fruit, but he was not referring to me."

Eve looked at him questioningly as he continued. "My beautiful Eve, you are the most beautiful creature I have ever seen on this earth. You are a goddess, a queen, a beautiful treasure to behold. You must not limit yourself to the touch of a mere man. Let me show you what you are meant to have. It will be our little secret. I can assure you. Can you not see that I am made for your pleasure?"

The woman was repulsed by the homely little snake but was flattered by his compelling and fawning words. Eve was still not convinced that the snake was being truthful, but even so she was listening to every word he said. She looked around to be sure Adam was not returning from his walk.

"Your father would not have made me and put me here in this splendid garden, in your presence, unless he wanted our union to take place. Why, we are the very best of friends, he and I. He even whispers to me that it would be sinful if we did not find pleasure in each other. This is the truth."

Eve looked closely at the unattractive snake and didn't see much there that would tempt her to be unfaithful to Adam. Still, she didn't want to hurt the poor creature's feelings. "Please, I beg of you, do not tempt me any longer. I am very content with Adam and he is my husband."

"You would be much happier with me, dear Eve. I assure you of this. Here, let me show you."

Frank watched as the snake's modest and colorless body grew thick and muscular, his scales began glistening like brilliant diamonds in the sun. Frank became mesmerized by the transformation.

The large serpent slid down the branch and rested his head on Eve's shoulder as his long tongue flicked, encircled and squeezed her breasts. Eve struggled to control her breathing. He then slid down and around her breasts and her waist.

"Look at me now, Eve. Am I not beautiful like you? Do you see how strong and virile I am? Don't be afraid of me, Eve. Touch me as you would touch your man."

Eve was enchanted by the beautiful serpent and she did as she was told. Adam was her husband and she knew no other, but he didn't flatter or praise her like this beautiful serpent did and he didn't speak of promised pleasures to her. What could these pleasures be? Anyway, it would be a secret. The serpent said so. She would resist the serpent no longer. After all, if Father wanted it, who was she to disobey him?

Her breathing grew deeper and heavier. Whispering to her all the while, the serpent's colorful scales brushed against the sensitive areas of her body and his tongue slithered between her legs. His compelling golden eyes rested on Eve's face from time to time as both ends of his thick body caressed her with an increasing boldness.

Eve moaned and gradually lowered herself to the ground beneath the tree. The serpent made a hissing sound of pleasure as he slowly penetrated the woman. He settled himself in tightly and began to move his body in and out, around and around, in a great display of obscene triumph. She gasped with ecstasy, threw her head back and closed her eyes. "Oh sir, I have never felt like this before. What are you doing to me?"

"I am merely giving my goddess what she deserves. Are we not inspiring together, my darling Eve? Your body is made for pleasure and I live to humbly satisfy your yearning. Lust is just another word for love. Lust is pleasure. Lust will give you great knowledge. Do not be ashamed. For there is no shame between the two of us."

Eve writhed around on the soft ground and responded slavishly to all of the sensations of her body. The serpent watched her with his golden eyes and hissed with satisfaction while he continued his seduction. "Beautiful Eve, do you want me to move faster?"

"Yes."

"Deeper?"

"Yes."

"Just there?"

"Oh, yes."

"Yes-s-s. I can give you whatever your beautiful body desires. All you need to do is ask and it is yours."

"Please!"

"Ah-h-h-h, do you love me?"

"Yes."

"Say it."

"I-I love you."

"And do you lust for me, Eve? Am I all that you desire?"

"Yes. I-I lust for you."

"I am bigger and stronger than your man. I can fill and pleasure your body all day and all night. All you need to do is ask, Eve. Give me your love. Give yourself to me and I will give you my lust. Tell me that you love me, my sweet goddess."

The serpent continued with his profane and limitless dance into his sick realm of evil, introducing the naive woman to the carnal indulgence she was never meant to have. And, once she felt the sensation, she would want them again and again.

While Eve's moans of forbidden ecstasy continued to echo through Frank's ears, he turned around, shamefully aroused, and crept quietly away. *What kind of dream is this? Is this really in my head or is someone putting these thoughts there. I can't tell anymore. Why am I having these dreams?*

•

A whispering voice cried, "Frank. Frank, are you awake?"

Frank opened his eyes and rolled over when he heard Karen's voice calling out to him. He was groggy and extremely weak but managed to sit up. He replied, "I'm awake now, Karen. How are you doing over there?"

"I'm in a lot of pain, Frank. I don't know what that bastard did to me but it really hurts. I can hardly move at all."

Clearly, Frank was able to sympathize with her because he could feel his own pain. "I know that it hurts, Karen, and I know that you're tired but we have to be strong. We can't let this exhaustion get to us and take control again." *I'll try to stay positive for her sake.*

Karen stated, "I don't know if I'm strong enough but I'm going to try to push myself towards the sound of your voice."

"No. Try to move away from my voice. I know there's got to be a door over there near you somewhere. Roll over onto your stomach and push as hard as you can with your arms. I'll try to move closer to you."

Frank wanted to share the strange dreams he'd been experiencing but didn't know how to raise the subject. Besides, he was trying to convince himself that they weren't all that significant. And furthermore, he didn't have the energy right now to focus on the dreams.

He could hear Karen whimper as she fought to move her body across the basement floor. Then, there was no noise at all. "Karen? I can't hear you anymore. Did you find the door?"

He heard nothing from her. "Karen? Are you there? Are you okay?"

Suddenly, he could hear the sound of Karen crying. He asked, "Are you alright?"

Her crying continued. "What's wrong? Why are you crying?"

"Frank, I don't think Eddie was the one who put us down here."

"Why not?"

"Because Eddie's in the basement too. He's a few feet away from me."

"How do you know it's Eddie? Can you see his face?"

"I can barely see him, but I remember that he was wearing a name tag. He still has it on. It says Eddie on it."

Frank was confused. If not Eddie, then who. "I thought Eddie was the one who put me here. Is he awake? Can you talk to him?"

"No, I don't think he's breathing. Oh, God. I think he's dead."

When she said that, Frank felt a sudden burst of energy. He flipped over onto his stomach and started to paddle his arms across the dirt floor. Going a further distance than he had gone before, he made his way to the middle of the room. Then, he stopped. He tried to locate Karen and Eddie in the darkness but couldn't.

He realized he'd pushed himself too hard. He rolled onto his back again. "But if that's Eddie, then who the hell put the three of us here? Who's doing this?"

"I don't know."

"Maybe that's not the bar above us. Maybe I've been wrong this entire time."

"Frank, I'm scared."

Frank and Karen could hear the sound of someone walking on the floor above their heads. Frank stated, "Whoever did this is the same person that's walking around up there. I have to get to that fucking staircase."

Frank was damned and determined to get out of there. He didn't care about the sharp pains in his stomach anymore. He wasn't worried about the overwhelming fatigue. His determination to get the hell out of that room far outweighed the misery he'd been suffering.

He flopped back onto his stomach again and pushed and pushed and pushed as hard and as fast as he could. When the pain got too unbearable, he turned onto his back and dug into the dirt with his heels to propel himself forward. It took a while but he made it to the first step, where he laid his head as he tried to catch his breath.

"Frank, what's going on over there? You're making a lot of noise."

Still breathing heavily, he said, "I made it. I made it across the room, Karen. I'm at the bottom of the steps."

Karen commented, "If you're in the same shape that I'm in, you're never going to make it up a set of steps." *I wish she'd try to be a little more positive.*

"I still have to try. I may not make it but at least I'll know that I tried."

With sincere concern in her tone, Karen let out a breath and whispered, "Good luck, Frank. I hope you make it."

"Thank you." Frank lifted his head and put his hands on the back of the second step. He hoisted himself up into a sitting position and parked his butt down on the step. He vaguely remembered the fun he'd had when he and his sister were small children ascending and descending stairs on their padded bottoms. The memory would have comforted him had he not been in such awful circumstances. *Oh, Marjorie, I miss you. I miss you so much.*

"How are you doing, Frank?"

"I'm doing my best." He pulled himself up to the third step, using his strong leg muscles to balance and support himself.

Then slowly, he did the same with the fourth step. He could feel his abdomen twist and cramp up more but he could rest briefly on each stairstep. He let her know, "Now, I'm on the fourth step. I really think I can do this."

Karen questioned, "How many steps are there, Frank?"

Frank looked up and noticed the light that had been peeking out from under the door before. He counted the steps. "It looks like there might be fifteen more to go."

"That's a lot of steps, Frank."

"I'm going to do it. It might take me a while but I swear I'm going to get up these goddam steps, even if it kills me." *The way I'm feeling, it probably will kill me.*

Frank put his hands on the back of the sixth step and hoisted himself up onto the fifth step. "Got up one more step."

He repeated this maneuver again and again until he was well up the staircase. He looked down at his distance from the dirt floor. "I think I'm about halfway there, Karen. It looks like I have nine or ten more steps to go." *I'm that much closer to freedom. I'll show them. They think they can keep me locked up down here. Wait until I get ahold of whoever did this to me.*

He didn't hear a response from Karen. "Did you pass out again?" *Come on, Karen. I need your support on this one.*

Still, there was no response from her. He waited a few minutes to rest and regain his strength as he reached for the back of the next step. His legs were giving out. All the strength he'd had moments before had drained away.

He laid his head against the wall and found he was completely overwhelmed with exhaustion. He couldn't push himself any further. He called out, "Karen, are you there?"

There was still no answer. He waited for a moment before he closed his eyes and passed out, sprawled on the stairs.

•

Frank discovered himself standing in the garden again. It was early evening and the clear sky was filled with brilliant stars. He saw Eve, pregnant and lying on a bed that was made of palm leaves. Every so often, the woman would cry in pain and her body would tense up as she got closer to giving birth.

Adam knelt at her side, waiting for the baby to come. He held Eve's hand and bathed her with cool water to ease her labor. He spoke to her gently, smiling and with encouragement as the labor pains continued.

Frank already knew that Adam wasn't the father of the child. He knew it was the spawn of an unholy alliance.

As Eve's labor continued, the heavens became pitch-black and ominous. The forceful sounds of thunder rumbled all around them. Bolts of lightning flashed and lit up the dark sky. The gentle animals in the garden became restless and agitated. The winds began to blow hard.

Adam gazed up at the skies and then around the garden and shouted, "I believe there is something wrong wife! Father is angry! He has created these conditions!"

Just then, Eve began to give birth. Adam helped and watched as the baby emerged from her womb, covered in a thin layer of shining snakeskin. Adam gasped. He was horrified. He recoiled from the baby. "What have you done to me, Eve? This child, this creature that you have produced cannot be my child! My child would not look like this! It has the scales of a snake! It cannot be my child!"

"It isn't," cried Frank. "The child belongs to the snake." But he was neither seen nor heard by the others in the dream. *They can't hear a word I'm saying.*

Once the baby was fully birthed, the scales shed quickly and left a newborn child that appeared to be human. The baby took his first breaths and cried loudly. He made a slight hissing sound as he cried. His eyes were a brilliant golden color. Adam had seen those golden eyes before. He knew. "You laid with the serpent! You betrayed me!"

Eve, who was completely exhausted from giving birth, grudgingly admitted the truth to him. "Yes," she said naively, "he said our father wanted me to lay with him. But I do not know if this child is from his seed."

But they both knew the truth. The serpent was the father.

Eve began to cry softly. "I am so sorry, my husband. The serpent convinced me that our father told him it would be a sin if we did not join our bodies."

"And you believed him?"

"I did not know I could bear a child from a serpent's seed. I was so foolish. I have never lied to you before. I will never do it again and I will give you children of your own. I will give you many sons."

Eve held the baby in her arms as she looked beseechingly at her husband, willing his empathy. At the same time, she remembered and longed for the serpent's touch, which she had already experienced several times.

Adam bowed his head, ashamed of his wife but still willing to forgive her sinful act. He knew that the snake was a powerful enemy, riddled with hate and cunning deceit. If he could find him, he would kill him "I will raise the boy as if he were my own. But you must promise to never consort with the serpent again."

Nervously, Eve nodded in agreement with her husband but ... deep inside ... she wasn't sure if she could keep the promise. The serpent was quite convincing.

A hard rain began to fall and the animals ran away from the garden. Frank watched as the panther slaughtered the sheep, and the hyenas surrounded a deer to kill. He saw the beautiful flowers, the magnificent trees and the lush grass begin to wilt and die.

He looked up in the tree and saw the well camouflaged and motionless serpent observing it all through golden eyes, smiling.

Frank thought to himself. *Then eating an apple from the tree of knowledge wasn't actually the original sin. Eve's infidelity with the serpent was the original sin. Adam pacifying her was just as bad in God's eyes.*

Frank felt as if he was actually there, all the sounds and smells. *Jesus Christ! What kind of drugs are they giving me?*

•

Dazedly, Frank woke up, opened his eyes and found himself, for the first time, in complete darkness. He could tell that he wasn't lying on the staircase anymore. He was lying back in the cold dirt again. *Someone came down here and moved me back again.*

The single dim dangling lightbulb, that had previously provided just enough light to at least see shadows, was turned off.

His gut and his side ached but he managed to find a way to sit up. For a moment, he thought about his latest fantasy and wondered why he was having such bizarre and vivid dreams. *I've never been a particularly religious guy, but holy hell, these dreams are hardcore fodder for an adult Bible study. I must have one wild imagination or is this some kind of mind control? Who's putting all these thoughts in my head?*

No matter. He couldn't be preoccupied with his dreams right now. He had more important things to worry about.

He strained to call out as loudly as he could but it ended up being nothing more than a faint and despairing murmur. "Karen, are you still there? Can you hear me? Karen?"

He was startled when he suddenly heard someone breathing heavily and then felt a pair of hands wrapping around the back of his neck. *Oh my God! There's someone else here.*

Frank froze in terror. His sudden crushing anxiety shocked his system such that he couldn't utter a sound as the warm hands progressively moved around until they were resting on the sides of his face and covering his ears. *What the hell are they doing?*

He feared, by the positioning of the warm hands, that someone was about to strangle him or break his neck with one forceful snap. Finally, he was able to say something, though barely audible. "Who are you?"

He didn't hear a word from the stranger as the pair of hands moved back around to the base of his cranium and unexpectedly began to rub Frank's neck. He could tell by the force and the strength of the massage that it was all being done by a man, a man with very strong hands.

Frank was confused. Why was he receiving a neck massage after he had been drugged, probably tortured, and thrown in a cold and dark cellar? He pleaded to the man that was right behind him. Frank cried out. "Please, tell me why you're doing this to me? To Karen? To Eddie?"

The powerful hands unexpectedly stopped the massage but remained resting there on Frank's shoulders. He was desperate for answers. He tried to reason with his captor. "I swear. If you let me and Karen out of here, I promise I'll never tell anyone about any of this. You can trust me. Your secret is safe with me."

Whoever owned the set of hands began to rub Frank's shoulders. Frank couldn't understand why his abductor was doing this to him. *It feels good and bad all at the same time. What is going on here?*

For a brief moment, a disturbing thought popped into Frank's head that, maybe, he was about to be molested in the dark basement by this man. He begged the man with conditions. "If you let me go free, I'll let you do whatever you want to do to me and I won't ever say a word to anyone. I'll be good. I'll do anything you want me to. Just please let me go afterwards."

The hands continued to massage Frank's shoulders. Then, he moved on to his upper arms and finally his lower back. Though Frank was in pain, hungry, dehydrated and sitting in the darkness, he realized that he was simultaneously repulsed and comforted by the massage. *That feels so good. He knows what he's doing.*

When the warm hands had finished rubbing all around Frank's back, he waited to see what was going to happen next. He could still hear the heavy breathing and feel the man's warm breath right next to his ear. The odd combination of darkness and the warm breath on the back of his neck felt strangely seductive to Frank.

During the whole time, Frank heard no movement in any other part of the cellar. Karen didn't call out to him at all. She didn't give him any sign that she was awake. He thought, perhaps, she was dead. *Maybe he killed Karen and that's what he's planning for me next.*

Fearing for his life, Frank began to cry. "Just tell me what you want from me and I'll do it. I'll do anything."

The man didn't respond. He just continued to warm the back of Frank's neck with his heavy breathing.

Frank flinched when he felt the man wiping his upper buttocks with an ice-cold cloth. Then he smelled an overpowering medicinal smell. He knew that the man was cleaning the site with antiseptic in preparation for an injection of the drug he had been given before. *I was right. He has been drugging me. That's the reason for all of the crazy dreams. That's the reason for all my pain.*

Frank cried out, "Please, don't do this again. I have a life outside of this place, a very good life, that I have to get back to. And I have a sister. I'm sure she's just one of the people who are out there looking for me."

The man in the darkness didn't respond to Frank's request. Frank felt the sharp prick from the needle. "I have money. I can get you cash. It's not a lot, but it's enough."

Frank didn't know what else he could offer to his kidnapper. He'd offered money, his body, and even his silence. That's when Frank realized that he wasn't there to be traded for money. He had been put in that basement for something far more sinister than he'd ever imagined.

The effect of the medication was almost immediate as Frank sluggishly said, in one more desperate attempt at freedom, "I can sell my house and everything inside it," before he closed his eyes and laid down on the dirt floor.

●

Again, Frank watched the scene, going unnoticed by the others in the dream. Darkness with brief flashes of lightning covered the skies. The boy was now six years old and the garden of Eden had become nothing more than a vast wasteland. Nothing was green and the soil had become dry and barren. Food had to be planted and carefully watered and tended in the thin soil. Even then, what was edible was stunted and bitter.

He heard Adam say to Eve. "You have brought this upon us. We have lived in misery and darkness since the moment of his birth. This decaying garden is our punishment for what we have done."

Eve looked down at the barren ground and said, "I know now that you are as right as you are wise, husband. We must find a way to correct our mistake." She looked at the boy with great concern in her eyes. Then, she looked at Adam. "I leave it up to you, husband. For you will know what is best."

The young boy, with gleaming golden eyes, looked back and smiled at his mother, exposing his rows razor-sharp pointed teeth. The boy was handsome, friendly and intelligent but these qualities had long ago been lost on the parents.

Furiously, Adam shouted, "He does not even feast on food! He survives off the blood of the small animals he finds, the same animals we need for food!"

Eve stood up. Frank saw that she was with child again. "I cannot have this baby while he is still here in the garden. I am terrified he might harm the newborn child as he does with the other creatures. He must go."

Adam marched around belligerently in a circle before he shouted, "Alright, Eve! I will do it! I will do what you ask of me, but only for the safety of our future sons! I pray that our father shows compassion and finds a way to forgive this unspeakable act!"

The boy turned his head and stared directly into Frank's eyes. The boy smiled gravely at him. Frank gasped and felt a cold chill running up and down his spine when he realized the boy, unlike Adam and Eve, could see him standing next to the dead persimmon tree.

Frank looked up and, once again, saw the snake's golden eyes shining down on them and then staring at him. Frank panicked. He closed his eyes tightly.

●

When Frank opened his eyes, he saw that the low-watt lightbulb was on again. His head was muddled as he tried to think back to what had taken place the last time that he was awake. He called out across the room. "Karen. Karen, are you there? Can you hear me?"

"Frank, you're awake. Thank God. I've been calling to you."

He was relieved to know that Karen was still alive and able to speak. "I just woke up. How long have you been awake?"

"Only a few minutes. This weakness in my body is really bad. I don't think I've ever felt this frail in my life. I'm so weak, I can hardly move. I feel paralyzed."

"Whoever kidnapped us was down here. I could tell it was a man and he was kneeling on the ground behind me."

"The kidnapper was here? Did you get a look at his face?"

"No, it was pitch black. He had the damned light turned off."

"Did he say anything to you, give you any clue why we're here?"

Frank felt a little uncomfortable telling Karen what had happened but he swallowed his pride and confessed. "No. He didn't say a word to me. He ... he massaged me."

"Massaged you?"

"Yes, he rubbed my shoulders and arms and then he massaged my back. I don't know why this happened. I thought he was going to do some other things to me but ... he didn't."

Karen's voice was hoarse. "I don't get it. The man throws you in a dirt basement and drugs you so he can massage you?"

"I don't understand either. But before I lost consciousness again, I felt him rubbing my lower back with an antiseptic wipe. I could smell the alcohol. Then, I felt it when he stuck me with a needle. At least we know that he's definitely been drugging us."

"This whole thing has me confused. If he's going to kill us, why doesn't he just do it and get it all over with?" Karen suspected what was going on but didn't let on to Frank.

"I'm just as confused as you are, Karen. How's Eddie? Did he ever wake up or do you still think he may be dead?"

"He's not here anymore. The space where he was is empty."

Frank questioned, "He's gone?" *He had to get rid of the body. He didn't want the evidence to be lying around.*

"When I woke up, I looked over there and he's gone."

Frank thought about it before he concluded. "He must have been dead. The kidnapper must have killed him and removed his body. So then, if Eddie didn't do this, who else would want to take us from the seedy dive bar and put us here?" *I dealt with a few loan sharks in the past but I always paid them in full and on time. No. No way. It couldn't have been that. Besides, loan sharks aren't kidnappers. They'd just break a leg or remove a finger and be done with it.*

Karen wouldn't tell Frank who she thought kidnapped them. Her voice suddenly got softer. "I can't stay awake, Frank."

"No, Karen. Don't do this to me again. You have to fight the fatigue."

"It just came over me all of a sudden. I can't keep my eyes open. Whatever this guy is giving me must be time-released."

Frank didn't want to feel alone again. He begged, "You have to stay awake so we can figure out what to do."

"I'm sorry, Frank. I can't …"

He knew that she was asleep again. It wasn't long before he was feeling the same overwhelming exhaustion.

•

With the phone pressed up to her ear again, Marjorie was frustrated, angry and worried. "I told you, it's been too long. My brother calls me every Monday without fail."

She stared out the window to keep an eye on the kids who were playing in the front yard. "Why do I have to come all the way down to the station to file a missing person's report? Can't I just do it over the phone?"

The kids had the hose turned on and were taking turns squirting each other. "Okay. Okay. Do I need to bring anything with me?"

Again, Marjorie could feel the beginnings of a headache. "I have pictures. I'll bring a couple with me."

She pulled the curtain open and shouted out the window, "Not so close to the street!"

Marjorie was more than ready to finish her conversation. Her frustration with her brother was mounting. "And even though I'm filing the report here in Boston, you're going to be able to check out Harrisburg? Thank you. I'll be down there in about an hour."

Marjorie stared out the window as the kids laughed and dashed around the yard hosing each other down. "Frank, this isn't like you. It's been too long." She feared the worst.

•

Frank abruptly opened his eyes when he felt the same warm, masculine hands on his back again, rubbing and massaging him.

Once his eyes could focus, he looked around and saw that the basement was in total darkness. He tried to speak through his dry throat and parched mouth. "Why? Why are you doing this to me, to Karen?" Frank needed to know what would become of him.

His abductor held a cup of water up to Frank's mouth and allowed him to drink from it. The water helped clear his throat. "What's next? Are you going to kill me? Are you going to kill Karen the same way that you killed Eddie? Is that your master plan?"

He could sense that the man sitting on the floor behind him was silently laughing while he began to rub Frank's shoulders. "What's so funny? Do you think it's funny that Eddie's dead, that you killed him?"

The man started to work his strong hands down Frank's lower back. Frank remembered that, the last time his abductor did this, he was given a syringe of some powerful knock-out drug. When he felt his captor's hands moving even lower down, he knew he had to find a way to stop him from sticking another needle in him. He made the man in the dark believe that he wanted more. He begged, "Please, don't stop. Not just yet. Would you just massage my back a little longer?"

He could tell that the dark man was excited by the proposal as his hands slid up Frank's back and onto his upper arms again. As the man rubbed Frank's arms, Frank continued to play along with the charade. He whispered, "That's it. It feels good. Just a little longer."

The man moved around to the front and started to massage Frank's chest. Frank continued to act as if he was deriving some sexual pleasure from it. "Thank you. You don't know how good it feels when you're doing that. I wish I could do the same for you."

The hands stopped moving for a moment. It was as if he was thinking about what Frank just said and contemplating just how good it might feel if the two of them switched positions.

Soon, the hands were moving again, all the way down to Frank's stomach. Then, abruptly he felt the stranger's hands move from his stomach and up to his face. His captor was thoughtfully rubbing Frank's forehead and cheeks, knowing all the right spots to give pleasure. And, strangely enough, Frank gave in to the soothing sensations, because it did feel pleasurable. Quite pleasurable.

Frank mentally shook himself out of the stupor and tried to think of what to do next. Should he just let the man give him his shot and go back to sleep or should he find a way to challenge his abductor?

When the man's hands steadily moved down around Frank's mouth and chin, Frank opened his mouth and bit the man with great force on the side of his hand. He bit as hard as he could. He didn't care about the consequences.

The man immediately jerked back and his deep voice shouted, "No!"

Frank knew the wound he caused was deep. He could taste the man's blood on his tongue. Then, without warning, Frank felt a heavy fist smashing against his mouth. With that, Frank could taste his own blood on his lips.

The same powerful fist punched him in the side of the head, and then again, and again. He felt the back of an open hand slapping him hard against his cheek and his ears. This caused Frank's ears to start ringing.

Frank fell over onto the cold dirt floor. He was confused and bleeding. Unexpectedly, a sharp needle was carelessly jabbed into his arm. The stick of the needle was even more painful than the slaps and the punches.

Frank could feel his eyelids were growing heavy. Before he finally passed out, he felt a hard kick to the stomach when his abductor decided he wasn't finished punishing him.

●

Frank found himself standing alongside the bank of a mighty river. He checked over his body and knew that it was just a dream because he wasn't bruised or bleeding from the beating that he had just been subjected to. *At least I don't have any pain in my dreams.*

On the other side of the raging waters, he could see Adam dragging the six-year-old boy by his feet. The boy shouted, "Father, stop! You are hurting me! Please stop!" *What in the hell is Adam planning to do?*

Adam continued to ignore the boy's pleas as they arrived at the edge of a tall cliff, a cliff that overlooked the river. "Shut up, boy. I am not your father!"

The boy looked up at Adam in horror when he began to realize what was in store for him. Without saying a word, Adam lifted the boy over his head and tossed him into the powerful waters. Then he stood and watched stoically with a sense of relief as the boy was swept away in the raging waters.

Frank was positioned, on one side and Adam, on the other, watched as the frightened boy flapped his arms and legs to keep from going under.

Frank ran along the bank and knelt down at the edge of the river as the boy was about to pass him. In an extreme effort to save the boy's life, Frank extended his arm and tried to grab the boy but he couldn't reach. He called out,

"Take my hand! Take my hand!" But he couldn't reach him.

Frank almost fell into the water and had to shuffle backwards on the bank to find safety. The boy with the golden eyes glanced quickly into Frank's eyes. Not making a sound, the boy swept past him as the mighty current propelled him along. The forceful rage of the river seemed to intensify.

The boy continued to go down the river, going under and then resurfacing several times until eventually he didn't resurface again. *He's dead. Adam killed him.*

Suddenly, the dark clouds rolled away and the flashes of lightning subsided. Adam stared down at the river and then up at the clear blue skies. He nodded his head and said, "It is good. We have been forgiven."

Frank observed Adam as he sauntered away with a look of great relief on his face. He displayed no emotion at the fact that he had just murdered a six-year-old boy.

•

When Frank opened his eyes, he knew the dream was over because he could feel the intense pain from the thrashing he'd received before. Frank didn't know how much time had elapsed since he had been battered by his abductor, but he did know that the agony was still fresh.

He didn't care. He knew that, in order to have received such a severe beating, he must have really injured his kidnapper. *Good for me, Frank. That makes me feel a little better. I just hope that asshole bled out.*

From across the basement, he heard, "Frank, will you please wake up?"

It was Karen's soft voice calling out to him again. "Karen? You're awake. How long have you been awake?"

"I've been talking to you for a long time, maybe an hour."

He strained to roll over but the pain in his abdomen was powerful. He remained on his back. Karen could hear him struggling to move. "How are you doing?"

Already out of breath, he muttered, "Not too good, Karen. I think I've had better days. How are you doing?"

Karen's voice was weak. "My whole body feels tender, like I have bruises all over me. I don't know how I would have gotten them. Wouldn't I have felt it if someone hit me?"

"It depends on how powerful the stuff is that he's injecting you with."

"It hurts. It hurts so much that I can hardly move. How are you?"

Frank chuckled, causing fiery pain to shoot through his stomach muscles. "Oh, I'm in pretty bad shape, Karen. He beat me up too but I was awake for the whole goddam thing."

"He beat you up?"

"He punched me, slapped me and he even kicked me in the stomach. He did it because I bit his hand. I could taste blood on my tongue. I'm sure I hurt him pretty bad."

Sounding positive but worn out, Karen said, "Good for you, Frank. Good for you. I hope it hurt him a lot."

Frank suddenly had an unhappy thought. "I'm sure that's why he beat you up too. Hurting you must have been part of my punishment. I'm sorry he did that to you."

He waited for a moment and didn't get a response from Karen. He managed to get up on his elbows and apologetically call out, "Karen, I said I'm sorry about what happened to you. It was my fault he did that."

She didn't respond to him. He called out to her again. "Are you there?"

After waiting several minutes for her to say something, Frank questioned, "Karen. Karen, what happened to you? You're not talking. Did you fall asleep again?"

In a low, muddled tone, she responded, "No, Frank, I'm here."

"Why didn't you answer me?"

"I was just thinking, Frank," she said in a low-spirited melancholy tone.

Frank grunted when he tried to sit up. "And what were you thinking about?"

"I was just wondering about the big world outside this fucking prison cell, and what's going on with my kids and my job."

"You have children?"

Suddenly, her voice took on a happy note. "Oh yes. I have a little boy. His name is Ezra. He's six. I have a little girl and her name is Emily. She just turned four. They're both beautiful. I miss the two of them so much."

"I'm shocked, Karen. You never mentioned that you had children."

"I had them young. I got married to my high school sweetheart, Jeff White, just a few days after our graduation."

"That is young."

"We had Ezra about six months later, and things went pretty well for a while. We both found good paying jobs, bought a house, and then Emily came along."

Frank was curious to hear her story. "What happened?"

"The usual. You know how it goes. We started to fight about money and other things. Then, the jerk went out and found himself a girlfriend. That went on for a couple of years until I finally found out about her and filed for divorce. And now, he's just another one of those deadbeat dads and I have to work two jobs in order to make ends meet every week. End of story."

"I just don't get it. I don't understand why some men think that they don't have to pay for their own children."

"He'll pay for them soon. I've been going through the courts and suing him for child support. It looks like I'm going to get everything that I asked for. My lawyer said that he plans on taking Jeff to the cleaners."

"What about family? Don't you have any family to help you?"

"No, I don't. My father disappeared from my life when I was five. My mother turned into the town drunk after he left. I remember picking her up off the kitchen floor on more than one occasion. She passed away a few years ago. I was an only child, so I don't have brothers or sisters. I've been on my own since the divorce."

"I think you'll do well, Karen. You seem like a good person."

"What about you, Frank?"

"What about me?"

"Are you married, any children?"

"No, not me. I've always been too much of a workaholic to get married and settle down. I enjoy living the single life, no responsibilities. I guess it's just how I'm wired."

"So, you're all alone?"

"No, I'm not. I have this amazing light in my life, my sister Marjorie. We were born eleven months apart. She's always been there for me and I've been there for her."

"It sounds like you're close."

"We are, always have been. She and I have always looked out for each other and she is a very good person."

"What does your sister look like? Does she look like you?"

"No. She resembles my mother and I take after dad. Everyone comments on how beautiful and silky Marjorie's hair is."

"She sounds beautiful."

"Of course, she lives six hours away from me these days."

"Why so far away?"

When she got married, she and the husband packed everything up and moved to Boston and I stayed in Harrisburg."

"Do you ever get to see her?"

"Not as much as I'd like to. And I just want to be closer to her and my niece and nephew. I love

their tiny blue house with a big sign on the mailbox
that reads, "The Cooper Family."

"She has two children?"

"Benny and Alice. They're great kids and
they love their uncle."

"I bet they do. What's not to love?"

Frank's mind began to feel jumbled again.
He said, "I'm getting tired, Karen."

"So am I."

"I think you're right that these goddam shots
he's giving us are time released. It's like my fatigue
comes in waves."

"That's right, waves."

"I never know when they're going to hit me,
but they hit pretty hard."

"I know what you mean, Frank. I'll talk to
you when you wake up again."

Frank laid his head down in the dirt and shut
his eyes. He knew the next wave was about to take
over his body. *I'll never get out of this basement if I
can't keep my eyes open. I've got to find some way
to fight these drugs.*

CHAPTER TWO

Frank opened his eyes and found himself lying on a hospital gurney in what appeared to be an old emergency room. *This has to be another one of those fucked-up dreams.*

The overhead lights were bright. He was groggy and parched as he tried to speak complete words. Nothing was coming out of his mouth but garbled noises. He tried to lift his hands up from his sides but they felt as heavy as cinder blocks. His body was weak, so weak. *I don't this is one of those fucked-up dreams ... or is it? I can't tell what's real or not anymore.*

The bright lights were hurting his eyes. They were stinging his eyes. He wished he had a pair of sunglasses. Ironically, he wished for the darkness of the basement.

He looked up and saw two men standing over him. Both of them were dressed in dark blue scrubs and wearing protective masks and rubber gloves. The men were talking quietly to each other

through their masks but Frank couldn't make out
what they were saying.

Suddenly, he felt the gurney being wheeled
down a long, dimly lit, pale white hallway. Both
men continued to confer with each other as they
pushed Frank towards a set of elevator doors. Frank
watched the elevator doors open and he was rolled
inside, as one of the men pressed the button for the
third floor. He tried to speak again but couldn't.
*What's wrong with my voice? I can't get a word
out. What the hell?*

As they approached the third floor, one of
the men, the blonde one, noticed Frank was moving
his mouth. He leaned over and said, "I think he's
trying to say something to us."

The other man stated, "Who cares what he
has to say? He's supposed to be sleeping anyway. I
don't get paid enough to have conversations with
the patients."

Frank heard the man referring to him as a
patient. *Maybe this isn't a dream. Maybe this is the
real deal.* He thought, perhaps he had been rescued
and brought into a hospital to treat the wounds that
his abductor had inflicted.

He wondered if Karen had also made it out
of the dark cellar alive. He attempted to lift his head
to get a better view of just where he was going but,
as soon as he tried, one of the men put his hand

down on Frank's forehead and pushed his head back onto the pillow.

Frank turned his head from side to side and saw two other metal gurneys that had been parked on either side of his. He saw several other men and women, all dressed in the same face masks and dark blue scrubs, hovering silently over each of those other gurneys.

Just then, one of the men who had wheeled him up, leaned over, looked Frank in the eye, and said, "We're going to put you to sleep now. It's not going to hurt a bit and it'll all be over before you know it."

Frank began to panic but was too weak and exhausted to act upon his feelings. Immediately, many thoughts began to run through his mind. *What would be over? Why am I being put to sleep again? Is it put to sleep, or **put to sleep**? Holy shit! I don't want to be knocked out again. I can't take much more of this.*

Frantically, his mind began to race. *What if one of these men kidnapped me? What's the big picture ... what part of the puzzle am I? Why are they doing this to me? They should, at least, try to explain what they are doing to do to me and why I'm here in the first place.*

The blonde man approached him from the side. He was holding something in his hand. Frank felt the prick of a cold steel needle in his arm. Then, he could feel himself drifting off to sleep. As he was gradually losing consciousness, he heard the other man say, "Let's get the show on the road. I want to take a break today."

•

He woke up in the darkness again, feeling gnawing pain throughout his entire body. He had never considered himself to be a particularly tough man, but he was surprised at the amount of pain he had been able to endure since his abduction. But God, he wished the agony would go away. Frank strained to move a little.

Even though it was pitch black, he knew that he wasn't in the dirt cellar again. He could feel that he was lying in a bed, a hospital bed with a hard mattress. *Why am I out of the basement? What am I doing in here, in a hospital?*

But, if he was in a hospital, where was the patient monitor and the IV pole that should have been lit up next to him? Where were all the screens that should be delivering information to the hospital staff? *And most importantly, I want to know where the goddam television is!*

It was a room, but it wasn't a hospital room. There were no windows or even a call button for the nurse's station. He laid his head down on the soft pillow and waited for someone, anyone to show up with something, anything to kill the pain that he was suffering. *Where are they?*

Suddenly, he heard a noise, a bump in the night, or day. With no windows, he didn't know if it was day or night. He sensed that he wasn't alone in the room. He tried to make a sound come from his mouth but couldn't. *Was it Karen? Did she make it out of the basement too?*

His mouth was parched, just as it had been when he was being held captive on that filthy dirt floor. Frank swallowed repeatedly in a desperate attempt to moisten his mouth, but each swallow was pure torture.

Once he could actually swallow, he felt an intense pain in his throat, as though he had a severe case of strep throat. He reasoned that the source of the pain was from tubes that had been put down his throat while he was under anesthesia. *I guess that's how they're feeding me in this place. That's why I'm not hungry.* He whispered in a low and gravelly tone, "Hello? Hello?"

The aching throughout his body was so overwhelmingly intense that two words were all he could muster. He waited for a moment and listened but there was no response. He thought that, perhaps, whoever else was in the room with him was having the same difficulty speaking. He waited some more but still heard no one answer him back. *I hope the other person in the room is Karen.*

In desperation, he found the strength to say one more word. "Help."

Abruptly, he heard a weak grumbling noise in the room. It sounded as if there was another person was trying to respond to him. He knew, by the deep timbre of the utterance, that there was another man in the room with him. *It isn't Karen. Goddam! It's a man.*

Frank tried to roll around on his bed and perhaps find a way to knock something over and make a noise. He needed attention. But there was nothing to knock over. He tried to stretch his arms to feel if there was a bedside table or a nightstand close by, but his arms felt like they had hundred-pound weights on each of them. He couldn't even get them an inch off the bed.

Suddenly, Frank heard a door as it squeaked open and then shut. He could hear footsteps in the darkness but couldn't see anyone walking across the room. In spite of his time in the basement, his eyes had not adjusted to the absence of light. *I can't see a goddam thing!*

He could hear the squishing sound of rubber shoe soles on a tile floor as they moved closer to him. *Sounds like nurse shoes.*

The person, who had come into the room, walked over and stood next to Frank's bed. The person lifted his arm and exposed the inner side of his elbow. He felt the cold antiseptic being rubbed on his skin. He smelled that medicinal scent again. Without warning, Frank felt the stick of a cold metal needle that penetrated his vein. Trying to ask for help with tears rolling down his cheeks, he quietly begged, "Is this for the pain? Please help me."

The person in the darkness pulled the needle from his arm and carelessly let his arm flop back down to his side. No words were spoken. He could feel it when the person put a piece of cotton on the site of the puncture. Then, a long piece of tape was placed over the cotton.

As Frank began to feel the injectable take effect on his body, he heard the footsteps squishing across the floor and the sound of the door opening and closing again. He tried to imagine that he had been given a pain killer. He was getting groggy but the pain did not dissipate. He almost wished for sleep, but knew, instinctively, that he was in danger. *I have to stay awake. I don't know what they're giving me but I have to fight.*

He strained to fight as hard as he could against the effects of the drug that was currently rushing through his bloodstream. *I can't let them win. I can't let them win.*

He wanted desperately to stay awake. *I have to keep my mind occupied. I have to stay alert. If I keep my mind in check, these drugs won't be able to work.*

He fought and fought but, eventually, lost the battle and closed his eyes.

•

Frank found himself standing on another river bank. He watched as a blonde head bobbed purposefully in the water towards the edge of the river. He saw the six-year-old boy clawing his way out of the water and onto the dry land.

Frank felt strangely emotional when he saw the boy and he had to swallow the lump in his throat, so relieved was he that the boy had survived the raging river.

As the boy stood up and walked towards Frank, he began to grow taller and older. In just that short walk, the boy had aged into a sixteen-year-old young man and had grown over three feet taller. The young man's body was thin but curiously muscular in build and his skin had a slightly grayish pallor. *This can't be happening. How did he do that?*

As he watched, Frank continued to ponder how the boy had survived the raging waters. He was sure he'd witnessed the boy drowning in his previous dream, but clearly the boy hadn't drowned. Aside from the paleness of his skin, the young man had abundant energy and didn't appear to be injured in any way. It was as if the brutal banishment to the rushing waters hadn't fazed him at all.

Frank watched as the young man raced down along the muddy river bank, chasing small animals until he'd catch each one, bite into their bodies with his piercing teeth and drink their blood.

At one point, the pale young man with the gleaming golden eyes stopped, glared over at Frank and smiled, exposing sharp fangs in the front of his mouth. It was as if the young man was actually enjoying Frank's voyeurism and participation in these little episodes. Frank felt that same freezing chill running down his spine again.

When the young man began to walk towards him, Frank suddenly felt sick in the stomach, like he was about to vomit.

He felt an overwhelming panic and a great sense of urgency to escape from the bank of the river. He closed his eyes tightly, wishing he wasn't there. *Holy shit, Frank. Click your freakin' heels three times and pray for Auntie Em or the wicked witch or whoever ... Just get me out of here!*

When he opened his eyes, the young man had vanished into thin air, leaving Frank next to the river by himself. Frank shouted, "What the hell is this? Why am I here?"

•

Frank opened his eyes and saw that there was a tiny splash of artificial light coming into the room from underneath the door. He could finally look around and see just where he was. The light only provided a limited amount of illumination but it was enough for him to see that he was in a bare room with just his bed, his pillow, a blanket, and another bed that was positioned across the floor on the opposite wall.

He strained to turn his head. When he did, he saw that there was someone lying in the other bed. He could see from the outline of the body that it was a man. The man in the other bed didn't seem to be conscious or moving at all. He didn't know if the other man was even breathing. Frank wondered if he was dead. Then, he wondered again if Karen was dead.

The door opened and Frank saw a woman entering the room. She was dressed in white scrubs and a surgical cap and mask. Most of her face was covered by the mask. Therefore, he could only see her sparkling eyes before she turned and stood over the other man, shaking his shoulder and whispering, "Hey, come on, and wake up, Norman. It's time for your medicine."

Frank could hear the man's faint plea for help. "Please, no more medication. I don't think I can take it anymore. No more medication. Can't you see that you're killing me?"

The nurse chuckled and said, "Oh, Norman, why would you think that I'm trying to kill you? I'm trying to help you get better. My job is to keep you alive and breathing."

Frank observed the woman as she pulled a hypodermic needle from the pocket of her scrubs and flipped the plastic covering off, letting it fall onto the floor. She lifted the man's arm and stuck him with the needle. As he was jabbed, he flinched and, barely getting the words out, questioned, "Why are you doing this to me?"

The woman in the white scrubs dropped the used syringe into a tiny wastebasket. She patted the man on the top of his balding head gently, just as she would do to an obedient puppy. "There, there, Norman, you look tired. Sleep now."

Then, she turned and walked to the side of Frank's bed. Frank gazed up and saw the woman's eyes were a beautiful hazel color and that the little bit of hair that was sticking out from under her cap was strawberry blonde. She said cheerfully, "I see you're already awake, Frank."

Frank managed to whisper out a sentence to her. "How do you know my name?" *How does she know my name?*

"Don't worry about any of that, Frank. Now, it's time for your medicine. You can try to fight me like Norman does or you can make it easier for both of us if you comply."

Frank didn't want to fight or struggle with the woman. He didn't know what she was capable of. He was quite aware that she was in control and could muster a great deal more strength than he had. Knowing that following her rules might keep him safe for just a little bit longer, he dutifully lifted his arm for her.

She was astonished to see how compliant Frank was being. "Well, thank you, Frank. It makes my job a whole lot easier when you play along with the rules."

She turned her head to address the other gentleman. She raised her voice, "At least Frank's making my job here a little easier, Norman! You should take notes." Of course, Norman didn't hear one word that she had said to him. He was already sound asleep, snoring gently.

Frank didn't try to speak to her or Norman again. He couldn't. The pain was too intense. His throat felt as if it was on fire. He just stared up at the masked woman as he felt the drugs take over his body. They made him sleepy again. His eyelids got heavy. He closed his eyes.

●

Back in the garden, Frank watched as Adam and Eve held and coddled their newborn son with great pride. Their reaction to the birth of this son was a very different reaction from that of the first son.

Frank also noticed that the snake was still slithering around in the trees. It remained carefully concealed from the couple's view, observing everything they said and did. *Jesus Christ, it's that damned snake again. Why is he here again?*

In a strange new twist to his dream, Frank could hear the serpent's thoughts. The serpent was consumed with bitterness and jealousy, not because of the union between husband and wife, and not because of the new child. Not at all. He was jealous because he couldn't walk upright or run with his feet on the ground or see the world from a human's perspective. Those tiny legs he had were useless.

Even if his tiny useless legs did grow to be bigger, he would still be wedded to the land, not slithering through the grass, perhaps, but not standing upright either.

Of course, as a snake, he could hang from high trees and this was always useful for eavesdropping and for his own protection. But he was still forced to slither. How humiliating it was to be damned by God to slither on his belly for eternity.

Frank and the serpent watched as Adam looked up to the sky and heard him exclaim, as he held his son above his head, displaying him for God to see, "My son will be called Cain! And he will be a great leader, a tiller of the fields and keeper of the flocks!"

Frank found Adam tiresome in the way he spoke with such pompous certainty, and he bitterly resented the fact that Adam had tried to murder Eve's first son.

But Frank knew what would become of Cain and of their future son, Abel. He knew their first son was still alive and that poor Cain would eventually be labeled as the first murderer. The snake knew this too.

Frank knew that the serpent derived great satisfaction in the fact that his own son was just fine while Cain's actions would someday shame his parents and be driven out of their land. Yes, this pleased the snake.

The snake left the garden and never returned, knowing his work there was finished and that his own son would soon fulfill his own destiny. Perhaps he could convince his own dark father to do something about his slithering issue, the serpent thought. After all, he, merely a small and lowly snake, had changed the course of history through his own cunning and just a small amount of magic. His reward should be as great as the feat he had accomplished. Payment in the highest form.

Perhaps his dark father would allow him to walk like a man, but he wanted to be large. Large enough that men would fear him and run from him. Large enough that all the creatures would fear him and run from him. Oh yes, that would be good.

Or perhaps he could take to the air like a bird, but be greater than any bird that's ever flown. Great. Oh, the freedom. Perhaps he could fly and shoot flames from his mouth. All these thoughts made the serpent very happy as he slithered away from the garden, contemplating his next acts of wickedness and destruction against the human race. He only had to find a way to convince his father, and the serpent knew he could be very convincing.

Frank suddenly felt tired. Listening to the serpent's thoughts exhausted him. His eyelids were heavy. He closed his eyes and seemed to drift off into a very restful sleep.

•

Frank opened his eyes and it was pitch black in the room again. There was no light coming from under the door. He opened his mouth and called out, as loudly as he possibly could, to the man in the other bed, but his voice was still just coming out as a faint whisper. "Hey, Norman, are you there? I know your name is Norman."

He heard nothing back. "Hey, Norman, can you hear me?"

He waited for a moment, hoping for the slightest sound but there was still no response from his roommate. He called out repeatedly. "Norman, are you awake?" Nothing. He didn't even know if the man was still in the same room. *Is he even over there anymore? Maybe they moved him or maybe ... he's dead.*

Frank was both mentally and physically exhausted. He laid there in the darkness, wondering what was going to happen to him next. First, he was drugged and kidnapped and tossed in a basement, then he was massaged and beaten and, now, he was lying in a hospital bed where he was always left in complete darkness. And to top it all off, there were the strange dreams he'd been having. *There has to be an end in sight.*

He didn't even know how long he'd been a missing person plucked from the real world outside. *Is it a week, two weeks, a month?* Idly, he thought about The Twilight Zone and wondered if he was in it now. He wondered about Karen and if she'd ever made it out of that basement. He wondered about a lot of things.

Frank mustered all the strength he could as he struggled and gradually rolled onto his side. This gave him time to think about his hectic life before all of this happened.

It seemed as if his abduction had taken place a long, long time ago. He lay there and thought back to that particular Monday morning when the whole thing began.

•

Frank received a phone call every Monday morning with explicit instructions as to where he'd be driving that week. Like clockwork, his phone rang that last Monday at eight o'clock on the nose. His boss informed him that he'd be driving all the way to Baton Rouge and would be spending two full days at a sales conference there before returning home. *Not another fucking sales conference. I hate those things.*

Once he hung up from the call with the boss, Frank typed in the full address on his GPS and then, in frustration, rolled his eyes. *Jesus Christ almighty! That's another goddam nineteen-hour ride! This is the third week in a row he's done this to me! First, it's Lincoln, Nebraska. Then it's Tulsa, Oklahoma. Now, I have to haul my ass all the way to Baton Rouge. What the hell is this guy's problem? What happened to the days when I only had to go two or three hours away?*

As always, Frank hurriedly chugged down his one cup of coffee, then took a quick hot shower, packed a bag of essentials and hung two suits in the back seat of his car, threw his new laptop on the front passenger-side seat, made sure that his phone charger was plugged in, and got onto Interstate 81 south, aimed towards his destination.

When he drove out of Harrisburg, he stayed on his cell phone most of the time. His first call was always to his younger sister, Marjorie, to see how she was doing. "Hey Marjorie."

"So, pray tell, where is the asshole sending you this week, Frank?"

"He's sending me nineteen hours to goddam Baton Rouge."

"All the way to Baton Rouge? What a great guy. Doesn't he ever conduct any business closer to home anymore?"

"I don't know what I ever did to him that he feels compelled to send me further and further away every week. I think he plans these long trips just to piss me off."

"Seems that way, Frank. Maybe you should have a talk with him."

"I've tried. He won't listen."

"Then, maybe you should show him that he can't push his employees around like he does. You should just quit." Frank knew he couldn't quit his job. He really didn't want to quit. Even though his boss was a jackass and he had to endure long trips every week, the money was too good and Frank liked his job. He was really just blowing off steam like he did every Monday.

Not wanting to talk about work anymore, he abruptly changed the subject. "Anyway, enough of that. Let's talk about your life. How's Ted and how are the kids?"

"Ted's fine. He's always fine. Alice's soccer team made it into the regional playoffs and Benny's birthday is this weekend."

"Another birthday already? How old is he going to be?"

"Eleven years old ... and he's growing like a weed. Wait until you see him. He's grown over five inches in the last six months. He's almost as tall as me now."

"Wow! Eleven-years old already."

Marjorie agreed, "I can't believe it either. They're both growing up so fast. Where does the time go?"

"And what are your plans for today? A little housecleaning and then sitting on the sofa, watching soap operas and game shows?" Frank liked to joke with his sister because he knew she could never be so idle.

"I only wish my day could be so easy. No, I have to go into work and do half a day today. Then, I have to pick up both kids after school. I'll deliver Benny to band practice. Then, take Alice to soccer practice. Later, I'll retrieve them and feed them again, bottomless little pits that they are." Marjorie giggled. "Finally, I have another one of those long and drawn-out PTA meetings tonight after I clean up dinner."

"Holy shit, Marjorie. I thought my life was chaotic, but you win. Hands down."

Marjorie giggled again and said, "Some of my days are a little better than others … and some are worse."

"Well, it was good talking to you, sis. It's always good to hear your voice."

"Yours too, Frank." Marjorie paused for a moment before she said, "I want you to take some vacation days soon and come up to Boston to spend some time with us. It's been way too long and the kids really miss you."

Frank nodded his head. "I know it's been too long. After this week, I'm going to tell the boss that I need a couple days off to unwind. I'll come up to see you then."

"Good. I can't wait."

"I've got to go now. I'll give you a shout next Monday and let you know when I'm planning to head your way."

"Okay, Frank. Be careful driving. Love you and I'll see you soon."

"I love you too, Marjorie."

As always, when Frank ended the call, he immediately dialed his boss to confirm the address in Baton Rouge.

Most of the drive was just going down the boring interstates and then a few secondary routes, looking at the trees on both sides of the road for hundreds and hundreds of miles. Frank usually stopped at truck stops to grab a quick omelet in the morning or a quick burger in the evening, use the restroom, and head back down the monotonous road to his destination.

Once the sun had set, and Frank crossed the state line into Alabama, he realized he was feeling fatigued and probably shouldn't go much longer without sleep.

Always persistent, he pushed himself just a little farther until he could feel that his eyelids were getting heavy.

Then, like the shock of icy water, a new memory emerged. The night was getting dark and it was raining and he was getting tired. Frank recalled seeing the man in the middle of the road and the look of terror on the man's face, in his eyes. Frank remembered slamming into him but not being able to find a body anywhere when he went back to look. No one was there. Still Frank had felt as if he was being watched and the feeling frightened him as though he was in danger instead of the man he had hit with the car.

The sudden memory was so distressing and brutal that Frank didn't wonder that he was just remembering it now. He recalled that he intended to deal with it the next morning by notifying the local authorities or something. *But I never got the chance to report it. I wonder what happened to the guy.* He felt tremendous guilt.

He was exhausted and anxious when he saw a sign that said there was a town a few miles down the road. The name of the place was Collinsville and he turned into the tiny community and searched for a cheap motel.

Still thinking about what he would do about the accident the next day, Frank realized that the incident could now be deemed a hit and run. Wow.

Nothing like this had ever happened to him before. He couldn't think logically about it. In fact, he couldn't think about it any longer at all. *It's all just too much.*

Frank grabbed his overnight bag and his laptop and checked into the Collinsville Motel. Then, he unpacked what he'd need from the car, went to his second-rate room, got undressed and jumped in the hot shower.

The invigorating shower gave him his second wind. Although he needed sleep, he also needed to unwind and take his mind off the events of the day.

A brochure on the desk caught his eye. The bar across the street offered free first drinks for all motel patrons. He remembered seeing the tavern sign. "The Twisted Tail ... doesn't sound too bad." He knew he could use a drink. He said to himself, "Why not? I can go for a little while." Then, he got dressed, stuck the brochure in his pocket and took a walk through the light rain to check it out. *Dammit! It's still raining.*

He knew it was late and he had to be on the road first thing in the morning. He promised himself that he'd only stay long enough for one fast drink and then go straight back to the motel room to get some shuteye. *I have to report the accident first thing and then get my ass back on the road. I can't be late getting to Baton Rouge.*

He remembered meeting the tall, handsome bartender, Eddie. "Hi, mister. What can I get you to drink?"

While he was enjoying his first of several drinks, he never counted on meeting that stunning redheaded woman with dazzling emerald green eyes and gorgeous figure.

•

Frank rolled onto his back and wondered yet again whatever happened to Karen. He couldn't get her out of his head. *I have to know the truth about her, one way or another.*

Was she still locked in that filthy basement? Was she brought to the hospital like he was? Then, he remembered when Karen had told him that Eddie was there in the basement too, but she believed he was already dead. *If the kidnapper wasn't above killing Eddie, why wouldn't he kill Karen too? Oh God, Karen.*

Maybe she was dead and would only be a memory to him from that moment on. Frank figured the third possibility was probably the most likely scenario. He took a moment and mourned her passing. *Happy trails, Karen. I hope your next life is a better one.*

Frank wondered how it was possible for him to have been taken from that filthy basement and moved into a hospital without being conscious and aware of the transport. *Oh yeah, I was drugged big time. That explains a lot.*

It bothered him that he couldn't make the connection between the two places. The only thing Frank was sure about was that his brain was tired of trying to figure out what had happened to him or Karen or Eddie. His mind was always on overload. *I just have to control my breathing and try to clear my head. Maybe if I clear my head things will make a little more sense.*

As the night lingered on, Frank didn't hear anything or detect any kind of movement from the man on the other side of the room. He wondered whether his roommate was dead, unconscious or even there at all anymore. Without assistance from any injections or tranquillizers, Frank shut his eyes and fell into a comfortable sleep like he used to do before any of this happened.

•

Here he was again. By now, Frank was quite accustomed to inhabiting strange and unusual dreams. He knew they were bizarre because he was being injected with the "make a person crazy" drugs. Nothing seemed to surprise him. Everything that was once strange had now become the norm, as far as his dreams went.

Frank stood at the edge of a tiny village in the middle of a desert. He could feel the cool and cleansing chill of the evening breeze. He could feel the tiny particles of sand blowing against his face and body. *These dreams are always so real to me. I can feel it and taste it and smell it.*

The sun was down but it wasn't fully dark yet. This time, he was determined to observe and remember as much of the dream as possible. He walked closer.

A stone wall appeared to encircle the entire village. From his viewpoint, the enclosure didn't seem to be very large. Had he been any further away from the village, he wouldn't have seen it at all because it blended so seamlessly into the desert from which it had sprung. It was well hidden.

Frank walked cautiously inside the stone walls that protected the village. He paused as his eyes adjusted to the changing evening light while he looked carefully around. All of the streets were irregular and narrow, as if they were designed and built hastily by a drunken draftsman. The rustic structures that lined each of the haphazard streets appeared to be dwellings.

As he walked through the silent and deserted streets, not more than lanes really, he saw one building that was much larger than the others. It was three-sided with the front partially open to the street. The opening to the street was disguised by stacked lumber, but Frank noticed because he promised himself that he'd recollect every detail of this dream.

As Frank explored more closely, he saw many coffins grouped together in the back of a large building. *Strange. A warehouse for coffins in the middle of a desert?*

He turned back and looked at the other structures that lined the street. They were more or less uniform in appearance. Each house had one single window and door facing out at the narrow street. All of the windows on the houses had bars on them.

Frank walked up to one of the windows and peered in. Curiously, it was nearly total blackness inside. There was no illumination, no candles, no fires, no oil lamps, nothing. *Maybe this is an old abandoned coffin maker's village. I'm not surprised it's abandoned, way out here, in the middle of nowhere.*

As he focused and squinted his eyes in the dark, he began to see some slight movement. Eventually, he saw people. *People?* People who were chained together, sitting there on the floor, moving occasionally to find a more comfortable position on the hard-packed sand. *Oh, this isn't good. I know what that feels like.*

Just moments later, Frank heard some noises coming from the building that stored the coffins. He walked towards the building and entered it slowly. The coffin lids were rising, one after another, and people began to emerge from them. *Holy shit ... coffin people. Zombies maybe. This really isn't good at all.*

The boy with the golden eyes, now a handsome man, was the last to come out of his coffin. He was very tall and slender. He moved with a supple fluid grace that, at once, belied and revealed his power. He had a deep and melodic voice. "The hour has come for us. It is time to feast, my children."

Frank backed out of the room and crouched to the ground by the stacked lumber to hide as best he could as he watched the coffin people fan out and enter the small houses. They studied the captives as if they were browsing through cheap merchandise in a department store.

The frightened prisoners shrank away in terror, some crying out and begging for mercy. They released several of the people who were in chains and, without ceremony, they immediately bit into their necks and chests and sucked the blood from their bodies. The helpless victims screamed out from shock and pain before they gasped their last breaths and fell to the ground, dead.

Frank couldn't find thoughts or words for his visceral reaction. He was astonished by what he was witnessing – the brutal and single-minded dedication to the task of feeding. He was horrified at the complete indifference shown by the coffin people to all the human suffering they were creating.

As the golden-eyed man finished taking the last drop of blood from his victim, he looked up and gazed directly into Frank's eyes. The others milled towards their leader and gazed at Frank too. They knew he was there. He knew they knew.

Frank, crouched a few feet from them, and began to shudder when the man stood to his full height and fastidiously wiped the blood from his chin with a linen cloth. Then, he slowly put out his hand as a gesture of inclusion and gently asked, "Why don't you join us, my son? We welcome you."

Had Frank been able to summon lucid thoughts, they might have included, *Oh God, help me forget this nightmare. This isn't real. It's only a dream. A dream someone else put into my head.*

•

Frank was awakened as he was being taken down another faintly illuminated hallway on his old hospital gurney. As he fought to open his eyes all the way, he saw that his cart was being guided by the same two men dressed in dark blue scrubs. He tried to speak, though his throat was dry and the inside of his mouth felt parched. "Where are you taking me now?"

One of the men heard his weak whisper and leaned down. He said, "Don't worry, Frank. We're going to take real good care of you. You're in good hands with us."

Frank saw that he was being wheeled into an elevator and, again, the elevator was going up to the third floor. While the men waited for the rickety old elevator to move, Frank discovered that their names were Wayne and Glenn when they addressed each other. Wayne said, "I'm getting really hungry. Do you think we're going to get to take a lunch break today, Glenn?"

Glenn replied, "Don't know, Wayne. You know how busy we've been."

Frank wanted to say that he, too, had been very busy and that he was also hungry. *Where is my lunch?* Then, Frank realized that he wasn't hungry at all.

Wayne grumbled, "So, we're busy. Big deal. I can't keep going every day without taking a lunch break. I have to eat something, Glenn. You know I have low blood sugar." Wayne let out a giggle when he said this.

Glenn glanced down at Frank for a moment before he said, "Let's just get this done and then I'll find out if we can take a quick break." Glenn leaned over to Wayne and whispered, "And you don't have low blood sugar."

Wayne got loud. "Okay, I don't have low blood sugar! Big deal! I don't just want a break! I want a thirty-minute lunch! I was promised a thirty-minute lunch!"

"Okay! Okay, Wayne! I'll tell them that we need thirty minutes!"

Just when Glenn yelled back at Wayne, the elevator jerked to a complete stop. The jolt seemed to shut him up.

During the conversation between Glenn and Wayne, Frank was trying to remember all the dreams he'd had since he was first abducted. *The way the dreams are happening. The way they're telling so many different stories that must be connected somehow. There is some kind of mind-control going on. That's it! They're messing around inside my head and feeding me with a tube when I'm supposed to be sleeping. That's why my throat is so sore. That's why I haven't been hungry since I was kidnapped.*

The elevator bell rang and the doors opened to the third floor. Frank tried to look around but the long hallway had poor lighting and it was hard to distinguish anything. The two men pushed Frank's bed through a set of heavy wooden doors and into a room where Frank noticed several other beds, all filled with people.

Frank looked at the ceiling and saw that there were dozens of lights but only a few of them were turned on. He heard a voice that sounded familiar. "Thanks for wheeling him up, guys. I can take it from here."

Frank instantly recognized her, the nurse with the strawberry blonde hair and brilliant hazel eyes that had visited him in his room. He tried to lift his arm from the bed. It was a struggle but he managed to extend his arm enough to take hold of her wrist. She flinched away until his arm dropped back down to his side. "Please, miss, explain all of this to me. I have no idea why I'm here."

The nurse seemed annoyed that Frank had touched her and then had the audacity to ask her questions. Defensively, she said, "It's not my job to explain anything to anyone in this place. I just work here."

Frank couldn't see her face because of the mask and cap but, even though her tone was harsh, he noticed that her eyes were warm and showed a genuine concern for him. He wanted very much for her to like him. He smiled at her with as much charm as he could muster. "Who can tell me why I'm here?"

The nurse glanced around the room at the other gurneys and the other employees who were focused on their own duties. "No one is going to tell you why you're here. If I go to my boss and ask him to explain things to you, I might be the next one to get fired and end up being sent away from here. We wouldn't want that."

She saw a tear dripping out of the corner of Frank's eye and rolling down his cheek. His mouth was getting dryer each time he spoke. "I just want to know why."

She said warmly, "I'm sorry, Frank. It's not my place to say."

He managed to lift his arm again and take hold of her hand. "How long have I been here in this place?"

"I don't know. I just know that I've been working with you for about a week now. That's when I first saw you."

"What have they been injecting me with and why did they have me locked up in that filthy cellar for so long?"

She pushed his arm down and leaned over him. Her face was only an inch from his face. She became assertive. "Look, Frank. I don't know what you're talking about. I don't know anything about any dirty cellar. I don't know what happened to you before you got here. Anyway, I can't answer any of those other questions for you because I haven't been given the clearance to do that. I'm only a level two employee, not level five."

"Level two? Level five? I don't understand. Who can explain this to me?"

"Nobody. Nobody's going to take any time from their busy day to stop what they're doing just to explain this to you. You're a current priority to them but you still have no value here. Not yet. Can't you see? You're nothing more than an experiment to them, Frank."

"Experiment?"

"I can't say any more than that. If I do, and they find out I did, I could drop to level one and we wouldn't want that."

Frank was astonished. "Experiment?" *What kind of experiment?*

"That's what I said, Frank. Now stop asking me so many questions."

He continued. "So, that's what this place is? I've been kidnapped and brought here so you could experiment on me?"

She looked around again to make sure no one was listening. She noticed one or two of the other nurses staring her way. She leaned down and whispered softly, "That's only part of it, Frank. And trust me, you don't want to know the whole story. Not yet. Now, I'd really appreciate it if you'd stop drawing so much attention to me by asking me so many questions. I've already told you a lot more than I should have."

It was then that Frank realized he was going to die in this place. He thought, perhaps the filthy basement was just a holding place to keep people until there was an available bed at their hospital. His mind was beginning to put some more of the puzzle pieces in place. He asked, "What happened to the other people that were with me in the basement? Where are they?"

"What other people?"

"There was a woman down there with me. Her name was Karen. And there was the bartender. His name was Eddie."

"I don't know any Karen or Eddie. Maybe something happened and they never made it to this stage of the program."

"You mean they're dead?"

The nurse was beginning to feel paranoid like everyone in the room was watching her. She shrugged her shoulders and said, "That could be what happened, Frank. I don't know. I can't tell you anything. You know, you're starting to ask way too many questions."

Surprisingly, Frank grabbed her wrist again and asked, "What's your name?"

She flinched and pulled her arm away from his grip. "Don't ever do that to me again, Frank. If they see you becoming aggressive, they're going to tranquilize you even more."

He laid his hand back down at his side and said, "I'm sorry. I didn't mean to …"

"That's okay. Just know your place here and keep your hands to yourself."

Frank questioned, "And what's that? What's my place here?"

"You're just one of a hundred in line. When someone doesn't make it, they get replaced quickly. So, don't ever think you're anything special around here. As of now, you're number eighty-five on the big list."

Frank turned his head to the side and saw all the other gurneys in the room. Then, he stated, "I'm tired now," and closed his eyes.

She leaned down, close to Frank's ear, and whispered, "Cassie."

Abruptly, Frank opened his eyes and asked, "What did you say?"

"You asked my name. My name is Cassie. Short for Cassandra."

He smiled and whispered, "Yes. Cassie is a beautiful name."

"Thank you."

Frank wanted to ask her for food but then he realized he was completely exhausted and not very hungry anyway. He closed his eyes again and soon drifted off into a deep sleep.

•

Frank opened his eyes and found himself standing in his living room in Harrisburg. He saw that the house was just as he had left it. His dirty coffee mug was still sitting in the sink. *How did I get here? Is this another dream? Why am I dreaming of my house?*

Frank walked into the bedroom and saw that he hadn't made his bed when he'd left on his trip to Baton Rouge. No surprise there. Frank never found the time to make his bed or wash his coffee mug either.

When Frank returned to the living room, he saw his sister sitting on the sofa. "Marjorie, is that really you?"

"Of course, it's me, Frank."

Frank rushed to the sofa and sat down beside her. "I can't believe you're here. It's so good to see you, Marjorie."

"It's good to see you too."

Frank glanced around at the house and then he looked at Marjorie. "But if this is only a dream, you aren't really here."

"I am here, Frank."

Frank accepted that. He was just happy to be in a dream with his sister instead of that snake or those coffin people or drowning six-year-olds with golden eyes. He asked, "Why are you here, Marjorie?"

"I've been so worried about you. Ted and the kids are worried about you too. You left for Baton Rouge and we never heard from you after that. You simply disappeared. We had no idea what happened."

"I was kidnapped."

"Kidnapped?"

"Yes. And then I was thrown into some dirty basement below a dive bar."

Marjorie listened intently. "But you're not there anymore."

"No. They moved me to a hospital. I think it's a hospital."

"What kind of hospital?"

"The nurse told me I was an experiment. I was just one of many people that was being kept there against their will."

Marjorie appeared perplexed. "I don't get it, Frank. You were kidnapped so they could use you as an experiment?"

"Yes."

"But why you?"

"I don't know, Marjorie. Maybe I was just in the wrong place at the right time. They won't tell me anything."

Marjorie lowered her head and cried. "If they put you in a hospital and they're doing experiments on you, it means you're probably going to die in there."

"That's what I'm afraid of. I'm so weak and confused that I could never even begin to think of escaping from there."

"Then, I'll never see you again. Ted and the kids will never see you again."

Frank's eyes burned. "Oh God, Marjorie, I think you're probably right." *If this is just one of those dreams I've been having, then Marjorie isn't really here and I'm not actually speaking to her right now. This is just another part of their mind control game.*

Marjorie stood up off the sofa and started to walk towards the front door. Frank followed behind her and asked, "Where are you going?"

"I have to get home to Ted and the kids. It's a long drive back to Boston."

"But don't you care that we may never see each other again?"

"Of course, I care. But there's nothing I can do about it. Nothing you can do about it. You've already given up."

Frank became angry with her. "I didn't give up! I told you that I'm weak. They've been injecting me with drugs that make me so weak I can hardly lift my arms."

Marjorie was equally as irritated with her brother. She grabbed him by his shirt collar and stated, "I don't care what they're doing to you, Frank. You have to fight."

"Fight?"

"Yes. Fight them with everything you've got left to fight with. You're not a man that's ever given up on anything."

Quietly, he repeated her words and let the words make him stronger and clearer. He knew he needed to begin thinking of how to get out of that hospital and away from those people. "I have to fight them with everything I've got. I'll never give up."

Marjorie smiled knowing the message got through to him and Frank was always very good about taking her advice. "If you listen to me, you might have a chance."

"I'll do whatever it takes. I'll find a way. I promise you that."

Marjorie leaned in and kissed Frank on the cheek. "I have to get moving along. I have a house to take care of."

"But don't leave. Not yet."

"I have to go, Frank."

"Why? Why can't you stay here a little bit longer?"

She smiled at him. "Because you're about to wake up, Frank."

Frank knew that she had no choice. It was how this particular dream was intended and how it was supposed to end. He was comforted with her fragrance. "I love you, Marjorie."

Before she walked out the door, she turned back and whispered, "I love you too, Frank."

•

Frank opened his eyes and saw that he was back in his dark room. *What the hell is up with these goddam dreams? They're starting to feel a little bit too real for me. But, at least, that was a nice dream and I got to see Marjorie.*

He tried carefully to shift around in the tiny bed but his body ached and his head was pounding. He called out to the man who he thought might be there too. "Hey Norman, are you over there? I'd say good morning to you but I don't even know if it's morning or not."

The room was silent. "Hey Norman, are you awake?"

Frank waited a moment and then suddenly heard a faint whisper coming from the other side of the room. "Yes, I'm awake."

Frank was both surprised and thrilled to finally hear his roommate respond to him. "Hello, I'm Frank."

"I know your name. I heard the nurse talking to you. You already know I'm Norman."

"Do you know what's going on here? Why are we in here?"

The man strained to get the words out. "We were kidnapped, abducted."

"I know that, but I don't know why they kidnapped us."

"I believe we're being used by these people to take our organs and then sell them to the highest bidder on the black market."

Frank couldn't believe what he heard. He hadn't thought of the black-market theory. "What? But why? Why us?"

Norman swallowed several times. As some moisture returned to his mouth, he found that he could speak a little clearer and louder. "It's gotta be somebody. Why not us, Frank?"

Frank didn't want to believe the story that Norman had accepted as truth. "Do places like this really exist?"

"Yes, Frank, they exist and I've had a lot of time to think about it."

Frank wanted to hear what Norman had to say but also wanted to find a way to disprove his startling theory. "So, how does all of this work, Norman, since you've had so much time to think about it?"

"They take us up to the third floor and do all kinds of strange tests on us to make sure our organs are decent, healthy and functioning normally. Then, when everything checks out, they keep us in here until someone needs a heart or a kidney or whatever kind of organ is a match. That's when they come in and take what they need."

Frank suspected that Norman had no actual proof to what he was alleging to be true. "Have you seen others who had this done to them?" *I'll bet a million dollars you didn't.*

"No, not exactly."

"What does that mean, not exactly?" *I guess I would've won that bet.*

"I had another roommate. He was already in here when they brought me in. I overheard one of the nurse's telling this man that the injections he was being given were to improve the function of his organs and overall health."

Frank, being the bigger man, brushed it off. He was ready to tell Norman that the drugs were making him delusional. He didn't know how to say it without pissing off the man. "That doesn't mean they've been harvesting our organs. Jesus! I don't know where you came up with that crazy notion in the first place, Norman."

Norman stood strong on the belief that they would end up being organ donors. "Believe what you want to believe and I'll believe what I want to believe, Frank."

After what seemed to be an endless moment of uncomfortable silence, Frank asked, "How long have you been here?"

Norman had to think about it for a moment. "Who even knows how long … maybe it's been two weeks … or maybe a month."

Frank blurted, "I have to get out of here. I can't die like this." *I promised Marjorie I'd fight to find a way to escape from this prison, and goddam, I'll do it.*

"Good luck with that, Frank. More power to you. There's no way out of here. Besides, they have every one of us so drugged up that we can hardly even walk anymore."

Frank wouldn't believe that there was no possible escape from this nightmare. "I don't care what you say, Norman. I'm going to figure this out and find a way back home. I'll fight them to my last breath."

"Like I said, Frank. Good luck. Just keep me out of it."

As Frank tried to sort things out in his mind, he asked, "Do you think that we could maybe sway Cassie to help us?"

"We? What is this 'we' shit? I never said I was going to help you. I said to leave me out of it. And who the hell is Cassie anyway?"

"Cassie, you know, our nurse."

"Is that her name? I wouldn't know. That bitch only sticks me with needles and tells me that everything's going to be okay. She never bothered to tell me her name."

"I have to think clearly. I have to be able to focus my mind. Maybe there's a way to manipulate Cassie."

"Big dreams, Frank."

Frank was getting frustrated with Norman's beaten-down attitude. He'd been through the same horrible nightmare as Norman but still wanted to fight to find a way out of that place. "They aren't big dreams. Anyone in their right mind would want to find a way to escape this madness. I can't believe you won't fight."

Norman only laughed at what Frank had to say. He didn't respond to the comment as he rolled over on his side and faced the wall. Frank stared up at the ceiling and tried to clear his mind. "Cassie is the answer. She has to be."

He rolled over onto his side and whispered to himself. "Why am I even here?" *Manipulating Cassie might be easy. After all, I am one of the top salesmen in the company.*

Then he carefully rolled to his other side. "What did I ever do to deserve to be in a place like this?" *There has to be a reason for being here that doesn't have to do with harvesting my organs. But what is it?*

He rolled onto his back and stared up at the ceiling. "How am I ever going to get out in this condition?" *If Marjorie said I can get out of here, she's got to be right.*

His arms were strong enough that he could raise them to put his hands over his face and rub his eyes. "I wonder if anyone has ever actually been able to escape from this hell?"

His whispering was just loud enough for his roommate to overhear everything. Norman rolled back over and said, "One guy tried really hard, but I don't think he made it out of here alive. I know for sure that nobody has ever gotten out and lived to talk about it."

"And how would you know any of that, Norman?"

"Because I heard two of those orderlies bragging about it. They said that a few have tried to break out of here but never made it to the finish line. This one guy got out but never came back. They figured he died. They were laughing because they said he'd have been better off sticking with the program here instead of being out there to meet certain death. They were laughing about the whole thing for God's sake."

"How did he die?"

"I don't know. They just figured he died. He was on a dark work detail and that's all I know. It's all they said."

"I don't care what you say, Norman. I don't really care about the man that almost got away. I won't stop trying. I have to do something." *I want to be the man who did get away.*

"Do whatever you feel is necessary, Frank. I hope you make it. But like I said before, keep me out of it."

"I can't just lie in this goddam bed, waiting for some goddam doctor to come in and dissect me. My life is worth a hell of a lot more than that. I have a younger sister that I have to see again. I'd rather they shoot me in the head and kill me. At least I'd die with some dignity."

"Then, good luck, buddy. You're going to need it."

Unexpectedly, Frank shouted, "If you'd just shut your fucking mouth for a minute and give me a chance to think, I might be able to come up with a plan! So, shut up, Norman!"

Frank knew he'd made his point when he didn't hear another word out of Norman for the rest of the night.

Eventually, a woman came into the room. She was wearing the same color scrubs that Cassie wore, but she wasn't Cassie. This woman was much taller. She was olive skinned and had dark empty eyes. She gave Norman his nightly shot and then gave one to Frank. The woman never spoke a word to either man.

•

Frank opened his eyes. He was still lying on his hospital bed and waited a moment to see if he was having another dream. It was quiet. The only speck of light came from under the door. *I must be awake but it feels like I never slept. Is this a dream?*

Frank lifted his head and looked across the room. "Norman, are you awake?" He saw that there was no other furniture in the room. Norman's bed was gone.

The door opened and he saw several people walking into the room. They came over and stood alongside Frank's bed. He saw their faces without masks for the first time. *I know who they are even though I shouldn't. Goddam! This must be another fucking dream! What's going on here?*

He saw Cassie with her strawberry blonde hair and brilliant hazel eyes. Even though she was still dressed in scrubs, Frank could now clearly see and appreciate the outline of her curvaceous body. His pulse quickened as he fantasized how her body would feel next to his.

He saw Glenn with his wavy blonde hair and gleaming blue eyes. Frank was strangely mesmerized by Glenn's muscular forearms that were covered with golden hair. He wondered why he would feel drawn to this hairy man in such a way.

There was Wayne with dark hair, a beard and mustache. *I didn't know Wayne had facial hair.*

Then, there was the other nurse with the lustrous olive skin and the mysterious dark and empty eyes.

Frank found that he was able to speak without struggling to get the words out. "Why are you here? Why are the four of you in my room?"

They positioned themselves around Frank's old metal gurney and looked at him kindly. He felt no threat from any of them. In fact, he could sense a curious excitement and anticipation in their facial expressions. He felt it too.

Glenn replied, "We're here to make sure you're comfortable, Frank."

The olive-skinned nurse slowly pulled Frank's shirt off, over his head. Her fingers grazed and caressed his arms as she removed the shirt. Then, she began to stroke his face, lips, ears. As she ran her fingers through his hair, she murmured, "Is this relaxing? Isn't it good?"

Glenn placed his strong hands down on Frank's shoulders and began to rub. He rubbed in a circular motion on Frank's shoulders and upper chest, then gradually moved his hands down. His massage became more forceful as he rubbed and squeezed Frank's pecs. Frank was so flabbergasted that he could hardly catch his breath. *Oh, that feels so good.*

The olive-skinned nurse began to rub against Glenn and kiss him even as they both continued to fondle Frank.

As Frank was easily becoming a willing participant, Wayne and Cassie pulled Frank's pants down, over his ankles, and off his body. Cassie then bared her breasts to Wayne as he bent down and sucked on them. Cassie unzipped Wayne's pants, grabbed his penis and roughly masturbated him with her hand. Wayne enjoyed and encouraged the rough play.

Wayne began to rub Frank's feet, moving his hands up to Frank's calves. Suggestively, he allowed his hands to slide higher to the inside of his upper legs towards his groin. Frank became increasingly excited.

Then, Cassie climbed onto the bed and straddled Frank. By now, she, like the others, had divested herself of all her clothing. Frank tried to lift his head to kiss her, but she pushed him back gently onto the bed. He stared at her, spellbound by her beauty. Glenn restrained his arms as the olive-skinned nurse began to rub and lick his chest.

Cassie put her hands on Frank's stomach and massaged him, entangling her fingers in his dark body hair. She bent down slowly and then kissed his navel. Her tongue followed her hands as they inched lower and lower until they found and encircled his scrotum and began to squeeze and rub.

She found a spot between his legs and did things with her fingers that nearly elevated him off the bed. She kissed his penis and took it into her mouth for a brief preview of things to come. Then, all too soon, she raised up and began to massage his penis.

Frank felt Cassie's warm hands as they worked their way around the shaft, making him bigger and harder than he could ever remember being. She knew when to slow her touch so that he would not be pushed over the edge too early. He closed his eyes tightly and moaned in ecstasy.

That was about the time that Frank realized he was completely naked with eight hands fondling and invading his entire body. Those four sets of eyes watched him greedily and lustfully.

He didn't know it, but a fifth set of eyes, ancient and golden, also watched in satisfaction from across the room. *Goddam! This all feels so amazing! I've never had this much attention in my life.*

Cassie leaned down and kissed Frank. She kissed his face, his neck, his shoulders, and his mouth. All the while, she continued to rub his penis and scrotum with her hands. Then, she lowered herself onto him and began to move slowly. He felt her body clinching him tightly as he began to move in spite of himself. He had never felt such exquisite sensations in his life and he wanted to prolong them as much as possible. Finally, he groaned and said, "I think I'm going to explode."

Glenn, who continued to gently restrain Frank's arms, said, "Go ahead. Whenever you're ready, big guy."

Frank smiled with intensity and nodded. He wanted this. It had been a long time for him and he knew it was what he needed.

The dark nurse had partially abandoned Frank for her own pleasure and was bent over in front of Glenn, who had entered her from behind and was happily pumping away. She spoke, "This is your show, Frank. Let's see what you're made of."

Cassie began to move faster, clinching him in her body tighter than before. *Jesus Christ, it's been so long!*

"I know what you want, Frank. It'll always be here for you. This is exactly what you want. This is what you want."

Frank's breaths were rapid and heavy. All the muscles in his body tensed up and Frank was ready. He was ready! He could feel it! *No! No! No!* "Now! Now! Now!"

•

Abruptly, Frank woke up and felt wetness down near his crotch. He looked down and saw that he'd had a wet dream. *But what a wet dream it was.* He quickly tried to pull the sheet over the mess. He didn't have to explain himself to any of the nurses. *Goddam, that was a great dream! Why can't I have them all the time?*

Then he heard a woman's voice and the sound of her voice was very comforting to him. It was Cassie's heavenly voice speaking in a warm and gentle tone. "Well good morning, lazy bones. It's time to get your morning shot."

Frank looked up and saw her eyes looking down at him. He could tell that she was smiling beneath her mask. *Does she know just by looking at me that I fantasized about her?*

He smiled as he stretched out his arm as best that he could, trying to be compliant and hoping his obedience would eventually sway Cassie to give up more information about the facility. She held his arm when she gave him the shot. "There now, that wasn't so bad."

She laid his arm down slowly instead of just letting it flop back onto the bed. There was a brief pause, a moment of silence as she gazed deeply into his eyes and he gazed back. "What am I doing here, in this place, Cassie? Why me?"

"Why not you?"

"I've been kidnapped and tortured. What did I ever do to deserve this?"

"You didn't have to do anything, Frank. It all happened by chance. You were just in the wrong place at the right time. It's basically the same story for everyone here, even Norman."

"What about Karen and Eddie? They were in that basement too. If they brought me here, then they must have brought them too. I need to know if they're alright."

"I haven't had any time to find out about what happened to your friends Karen and Eddie. It's been a very busy week for me down the hall, in the lab. Besides, I work strictly on this floor and this floor only. They might have been brought in and put on a different floor."

Frank's eyes showed Cassie a true concern for Karen, and even Eddie. "Please, if you can find out anything, I'd appreciate it, Cassie."

She gave in. "I'll try."

"Thank you."

"But I'm not going to make any promises. If they see me looking through the patient files from a different unit … well … I don't want to think what they'd do to me."

"I don't want you to put yourself in any kind of danger. I couldn't live with that. If it's too risky, then don't do it."

"I'll be careful. I'm friendly with some of the girls on the fourth floor. They might be able to give me some information."

Frank suddenly felt the drugs beginning to take effect. He could feel his eyelids getting heavy. In a flash, he was asleep again.

●

When Frank opened his eyes, he found that he was able to stretch out his arms with very little discomfort. This shocked him. Did they stop giving him his injections? Was it true? Were the injections actually making him healthier? Why did his arms suddenly feel better than they had since … since the day before his abduction?

He remained quiet about his new discovery. He decided not to say a word to Norman or Cassie. Frank didn't know yet if he could trust Norman. As far as Frank could tell, Norman was a loose cannon who spouted off whatever he wanted and didn't care who overheard him.

He didn't tell Cassie because he knew, even though she had been kind to him, that she was still employed by the powers that be. Frank knew that, if it came down to it, Cassie would have to protect her job and herself.

He waited for Cassie to come into the room. "Good morning, sunshine."

"Good morning, Cassie. Is it really morning out there?" *Who knows what time it is in this dark prison cell?*

She shook her head. "It's actually two in the afternoon, Frank. I just said good morning because you've been asleep for almost eighteen hours. You must have really been tired."

Frank knew why he was so tired. It was the same reason why he'd always been tired. He'd been injected with their mystery drugs. He knew it and Cassie knew it too. It pissed him off when Cassie made light of the fact that he was being drugged. "How's your throat feeling today?"

Surprisingly, Frank didn't feel much pain in his throat either, but he didn't want to let on to her things were looking up. He rubbed the back of his neck and said, "It's feeling about the same." *Why should I tell you how I'm really doing?*

Frank was elated that his arms and his throat were better. Then he realized that the intense pain in his abdomen had also subsided. He celebrated these breakthroughs on the inside, not allowing Cassie or Norman to know about them.

Cassie mentioned, "You're actually starting to look a lot better, Frank. Your skin isn't as gray as it was before."

"My skin was gray? I didn't know that. How could my skin have been gray?"

Without any sign of emotions, Cassie stated, "Because that's the disgusting color your skin turns when you're a dying man."

Frank gasped. "Am I a dying man?"

And then Norman felt the need to chime in from across the room. "Of course, you're a dying man, you idiot. We're all dying in this place, but not before they harvest your organs first. They keep you alive until then."

Cassie looked at Norman and said in a humorous and teasing voice, "I wish you'd stop saying that we're harvesting your organs, Norman. Believe me when I tell you that no one would want your organs."

Frank chuckled at Cassie's comment. She turned back and said, "I can't believe I made you laugh, finally."

Frank knew she was sharing in the laughter beneath her mask. "Oh Frank, I wish all the patients could be like you."

Cassie decided to give Norman his shot first. Then, he might pass out quickly and stop talking of things he knew nothing about. Once Norman got his injection, Cassie came across the room and put her hands on the side railing of Frank's bed. "It's your turn, Frank."

Frank realized that his plan was gradually beginning to work. Cassie liked him and he made sure he continued to be submissive to her. He just had to make certain that neither she nor Norman discovered that he had begun to recover some of his strength. *I have to keep up this little masquerade for as long as I can.*

Frank knew that he'd have to exercise his arms and legs when Norman was asleep and when Cassie wasn't there. The strategy would be a slow process but he believed it would work. Frank felt a glimmer of hope. He was damned and determined to find a way out of the prison they had created for him. He remembered what Marjorie had said to him in the dream. He had to fight to gain his freedom. He had to escape.

Cassie gently lifted his arm and gave him the injection. He gazed up at her with a smile on his face before he closed his eyes and drifted off into another deep sleep.

●

Over the next few days, every time Frank opened his eyes when the room was pitch black, he noticed that his eyes adjusted to the darkness much faster than they had before. He felt stronger as he continued to exercise his arms and his legs. He even got to the point where he was able to sit up and get out of his bed.

His legs were still weak and he was only able to stand for a few minutes, but he stubbornly persisted. All the while, Frank kept it to himself. *This is my little secret for now.*

He was aware that letting Norman, Cassie or any of the staff know that he was making any kind of progress could be dangerous. It was all done quietly. *Come hell or high water, I'm going to get out of here.*

Just as he was getting back into his bed and pulling the sheet up, he heard Norman grumbling to himself as he was waking up. Cheerfully, Frank said "Hello, Norman. How are you today?"

"Fuck you, Frank."

Sensing that Norman was still feeling the intense pain that he, himself, no longer had, Frank tried to show a little compassion for a man he didn't like. "I'll try to ignore your last comment. I hope you're not feeling too bad today."

"Well, I do feel like shit. So, one more time, fuck you, Frank."

When Frank had first gotten to know the man in the other bed, he'd detested his habitual negativity. But now he'd decided not to let it bother him anymore. "Norman, we just have to make the best of this situation. Maybe there is a chance that we'll get out of here."

"You got big dreams, Frank. Keep telling yourself that."

"I'm staying hopeful."

"Good for you."

"You should try to be more optimistic too, Norman. It couldn't hurt to be a little nicer to Cassie and the other nurse."

"Why in the hell would I want to be nice to our prison guards?"

"Did you ever hear the saying that you catch more bees with honey than you do with vinegar? I've been nice to everyone and I seem to be getting treated better."

"I don't want to be nice. This place is going to be the last place I see before I die. Why should I be happy about that?"

Frank decided to give Norman a little hope to see if it would help. "When I leave this place, and I am going to leave this place, I promise I'm going to take you with me."

Frank heard Norman laughing. He laughed to the point where he was coughing. "That's real funny, Frank."

"Why is that funny?" *Jesus Christ, he's the most negative person I ever met.*

Unexpectedly, Norman's voice got louder as he yelled across the room, "We can't even walk and you're talking about breaking out and, to top it off, you're going to drag me along with you." Norman started laughing hard again.

"I just wanted to let you know that, if I can get out, I won't forget you."

"Thanks, Frank. But I don't know what your offer will do for me."

Frank didn't much like Norman but he did need the nasty man to be on his side. If he was to escape, with or without his roommate, Frank had to make sure Norman wouldn't alert anyone to what was taking place.

Frank was just about to get out of his bed and stumble across the room to show Norman that his plans were real. He wanted to make Norman see that an escape was possible.

As Frank pulled his sheet down and pushed it to the side, the door opened suddenly and Cassie came into the room with the needles in her pocket. The other nurse with olive skin and dark empty eyes came into the room too.

Frank exhaled a long breath. He knew that his little secret would have been discovered if he had gotten out of the bed a few moments before. He realized that he'd almost made a grave blunder by trying to pacify Norman.

Cassie said in a cheerful tone, "Well, good morning, guys. I see that you're both awake. I brought Rochelle along to help me today. I hope you don't mind."

Norman said, "No, I don't mind … like I really have a choice."

Cassie said, "I see Mr. Cranky is in his usual form today."

"I just woke up. Cut me a break."

"And how are you feeling today?"

"How the hell do you think I'm feeling? I feel like crap."

Cassie turned to Frank and asked, "And how are you doing, Frank?"

He smiled at her and said, "I'm doing okay. I slept all through the night … or day. I don't think I'm hurting as bad as Norman."

Norman shouted out, "Speak for yourself, Frank! I don't need you to come to my defense. So, mind your own business!"

Cassie said, "Wow! Somebody woke up on the wrong side of the bed today. Who shit in your Wheaties this morning, Norman?" She walked back over to Norman, pulled the hypodermic needle from her pocket and jabbed it into his arm. He flinched away when she did this. "There you go. This will put you in a better mood. Now, why don't you go back to sleep?"

He looked up at her and whispered, "Fuck off, Cassie." Then, she watched as he slowly closed his eyes and began to snore.

She didn't pay any mind to what he'd said to her. After all, she'd been dealing with Norman a while now and had grown used to his cantankerous attitude and filthy mouth. Besides, Norman wasn't the only difficult patient she had to contend with. They were everywhere.

The beautiful Rochelle stood silently on the other side of the room. She didn't speak or interact with Frank or Norman.

Cassie turned to Frank and said, "You're looking good, better and better each time I see you. He nodded. Then she asked, "Ready for your shot, Frank?"

He whispered, "I know it's been a while but did you ever find out what happened to my friends Karen and Eddie?"

She huffed. She didn't want Rochelle to know she had been helping a patient. She leaned down and whispered back, "I went to the second floor and tried to see what I could find out. There's no info on either of them. That means that they probably died before they could be transported here. That's all I know, Frank."

"Well, thank you for doing that for me. I know it was risky." He lifted his arm only a few inches off the bed, not letting Cassie know that he could lift it all the way over his head. He smiled and said, "I'm ready for my shot."

Rochelle walked to the edge of Frank's bed and said, "You've been so compliant with us, you don't know how much easier you make our job. I hope you do well here."

Cassie gazed meaningfully into Rochelle's dark and empty eyes and said, "He is my favorite patient. He's been compliant for me because I've been good to him."

Rochelle felt slighted by Cassie's comment. "I have other patients to check on." She turned and left the room. Cassie looked down and gave Frank a wide grin.

Frank saw that Cassie was a little jealous and seemed to be staking out her territory. *This is it. A window has opened and I can see my way out of this place. I just have to keep playing into Cassie's hands for a little longer.*

●

He saw it all. Everything. Frank stood there in that sleazy dive bar called The Twisted Tail, off to the side, and saw his entire abduction taking place.

"Nature calls." He saw himself gallantly telling Karen that he had to take a piss. Karen swung around on her bar stool and took a sip of her martini.

Eddie then came out from behind the bar and walked over to the jukebox. Karen sat there, staring at her drink, seemingly deep in thought, as she waited for Frank to return.

Frank appreciated her beauty once again as he observed her. But Karen didn't see Eddie walking up behind her and hitting her over the back of the head.

She lost consciousness. Eddie caught her before she fell off her barstool and dragged her into the back room. Then, he came back and cleaned up her glass and napkin before Frank returned from the men's room. *Goddam! I knew it! I knew it was that bastard Eddie! If I ever see him again, I'll kill him!*

Frank continued to observe, unnoticed, as Eddie finished what he was doing and stood behind the bar. He took a vial from his pocket, opened it and poured it into what remained of Frank's drink.

Frank observed as he returned from the men's room and asked about Karen. He saw the exchange between him and Eddie as he became progressively angrier at Eddie's persistent lies and attitude.

He watched as he took the last gulp of his tainted bourbon and ginger ale. He shouted, "Stop! Frank! Don't drink that! He put something

in there!" He watched in dread as he stormed
out of the bar.

Minutes later, Frank watched as Eddie
brought him back into the bar, propped him up
on the barstool and left him there while he went
into the back room again. Frank saw himself
slipping off the barstool and landing hard on
the floor. *No wonder I felt so goddam bad when I
woke up. Motherfucker spiked my drink and let
me fall off the barstool!*

Frank was horrified when he saw two
men coming from the back room with Eddie. It
was the two orderlies from the hospital. *Glenn
and Wayne? What the fuck?*

Glenn and Wayne lifted Frank off the
floor and carefully moved him to the basement.
After they came back up the stairs, they stood
aside for Eddie, who was carrying Karen down
to the same place.

Glenn moved quickly to the bar and took
out three shot glasses. He poured three shots of
tequila before Eddie returned. Frank watched as
Glenn took another tiny vial from his pocket and
spiked one of the shots.

Once Eddie had returned to the first
floor, Glenn smiled and said, "We did good. I
think we all deserve a shot."

Eddie was the kind of guy who would never say no to a free drink, especially a shot of the best tequila. He took the shot. Glenn and Wayne waited a few minutes until the effects of the shot hit Eddie hard. "I'm not feeling so good. My stomach. I'm getting dizzy, guys." It was then that Eddie realized he had been double crossed. He leaned over on the bar. *Perfect! Just give it another minute or two, Eddie, and you'll feel a hell of a lot more than that.*

Glenn and Wayne stood there and didn't say a word. Eddie looked up at them and said, "What the fuck did you do to me? I told you I'd do this for a couple hundred bucks. We had an agreement."

Glenn put his hand over his mouth when he began to chuckle. "And you did good, Eddie. We'll let the boss know that."

Eddie felt a wrenching pain in his gut. He knew he'd consumed the same solution that he'd given to Frank. "I don't ... I don't think ..." Eddie dropped to the floor and passed out.

Glenn looked at Wayne and asked, "Are you going to help me carry him?"

Wayne smiled. "Sure, but first I think we should call the boss and let him know the job is done, and then we should have a couple more of those shots."

Glenn laughed. "Okay, Wayne. We'll have one more shot and finish up here, but we have to be back to the facility soon."

Wayne elbowed Glenn and said playfully, "Don't spoil my good time. I want to savor the moment. After all, this seems to be the only way I can manage to get a thirty-minute break, if you know what I mean."

Frank couldn't believe what he had seen. He was drugged by Eddie. Karen was knocked out by Eddie, and then the idiot was double crossed by Glenn and Wayne. *When I'm better, when I can function like a normal person again, I'll take care of those two bastards. They won't get away with this.*

•

Frank woke up with a whole new picture of what was going on. He knew that he couldn't trust Glenn or Wayne after what he had witnessed in his dream. In fact, he was sure that the nurses, Cassie and Rochelle, were part of the plan too. *I just have to play along with them until I'm strong enough to get my ass up and out of here.*

He couldn't tell if it was day or night. He had been awake for several hours and his eyes were focused in the darkness. He heard Cassie coming

into the room while making her rounds. It was time
to put his plan in place. He knew his arms were
strong and he was capable of walking several laps
around the room.

He closed his eyes and pretended to still be
asleep when he heard the door open. He could hear
Cassie speaking to Norman and Norman spitting his
adolescent and boorish comments at her. Frank was
surprised when she said, "Norman, you're starting
to look a little better, just like Frank."

"Big goddam deal, Cassie."

Frank listened and waited. He could hear the
squishing of her shoes on the white tile floor as she
approached Frank's bed.

Believing that he was asleep, she took the
needle from her pocket and was about to give him
his shot when he quickly raised up his arm, swung it
out and knocked the needle from Cassie's hand. The
glass vial hit the floor and smashed. Frank did what
he'd intended to do.

She looked at him and assumed that he must
have been dreaming. She grabbed a small towel
from her pocket and knelt down on the floor. "What
a mess."

As she was cleaning the glass and liquid off
the floor, Frank opened his eyes, lifted his head and
looked down. Cassie looked up as Frank saw the
smear of dark red liquid on the floor. It was blood!

There was blood in the vial? Why is there blood in the goddam vial?

Frank played dumb. "What happened? Why are you on the floor, Cassie?"

"I was about to give you your shot but you moved and knocked the needle out of my hand. It hit the floor and shattered."

Frank continued to stare at the blood on the floor while Cassie cleaned it up. She knew he'd seen something he shouldn't have. "Frank, I don't want to hear anything about what was in that vial. It's not what you think."

Actually, Frank didn't think anything. He was clueless as to why Cassie would be injecting him with blood. He knew he had to pretend that he had a theory in order to pull the real truth from Cassie. "I know what I saw, Cassie. I can't believe that's your big secret."

She finished wiping the floor before she stood up and said, "You don't understand, Frank. What we're doing will save our kind. We're a dying breed and this is going to save us." *What the hell is she talking about?*

Frank was completely confused with the conversation. He needed to know more. "What breed are you talking about?"

"Our breed ... my breed ... my race."

"And how are these injections going to help you exactly?"

"Our race will be replenished. We'll have a chance to repopulate."

"Repopulate? Repopulate what?"

Cassie shrugged her shoulders and shook her head. "Never mind, Frank. I think I already told you way too much. Remember, I told you I'm only level two. It's not my place."

"You told me things but they don't make any sense, Cassie."

"They don't have to make sense to you. As long as they make sense to me."

Frank could see that Cassie was upset that she had broken a vial of the precious blood. She looked at Frank and said, "You need to get your injection for tonight but I have to leave this ward now."

Frank smiled and asked, "When do you think you'll be back?"

"I won't be back tonight. I'll find Rochelle or one of the men and send them down in a little while. One of them can give you your shot. I have other patients to see."

Cassie turned and, without another word to Frank, left the room. He could see that she was truly bothered by the whole incident.

Once she'd left, Frank waited for someone to come back with a shot. But after an hour or so, nobody came. *Cassie must have told them and they forgot, or she forgot to tell them. Whatever ...* He was glad. He didn't want to see anyone. He didn't trust any of them.

Hours later, Frank closed his eyes and, for the first time in a long time, went to sleep without the assistance of blood.

•

In the days that followed, Frank continued to exercise when he could do so without being found out. He noticed that Norman had started to look and feel better too. "Good morning, Norman. How are you doing today?"

"Actually, I'm feeling okay. The pain in my stomach is hardly there anymore and my throat feels clear. I don't get it."

"Get what?"

"For the longest time, I was in all of this horrible pain. My gut felt like I swallowed a couple pounds of sharp rock and my throat was raw and sore. Real sore. Like scratch and bleed sore. And I was really weak. But now, I feel like I'm finally getting some strength back."

Frank knew that Norman was improving just as he had begun to do a week before. "I'm happy to hear that, Norman."

"And what about you, Frank? How are you feeling today?"

"I feel okay today."

Norman shocked Frank when he spilled the beans. "Don't you feel like getting up and taking a walk around the room?"

Frank didn't know what to say. He knew he had been caught. He questioned nervously, "What are you talking about?"

"You know what I'm talking about, Frank. I saw you."

"You know I can't get up and walk?"

"Now, come on, Frank. I've watched you get out of that bed and practically jog in circles for a week now."

Apprehensively, Frank laughed. "You must have been dreaming that."

"No. I was wide awake but you just didn't know I was awake."

Frank realized he had to fess up and tell the truth to his roommate. "Okay. Here's what's been happening. I've been feeling better for a week, the same way you're feeling now. I've been exercising my arms and legs because I do plan to go out that door one day soon."

Finally, Norman began to show a hint of optimism in his voice. "Maybe I should start doing the same thing, exercising."

"You could."

"Then, maybe the two of us could get out of here together."

Frank was excited to hear that his roommate had finally crossed over to his side. "I told you that I was taking you with me."

"I know you did. I'm really sorry that I've been such a stubborn asshole to. It was all the pain and misery talking. I'm not that kind of guy. I am a good guy … really."

This was big! Real big! Frank was thrilled and delighted that he and Norman were beginning to reach some mutual understanding. By no means did they have all the facts about their situation, but they might just be able to talk sensibly without squabbling like children.

Still, he didn't want to tell Norman that he was being injected with blood every day. He didn't know how he'd handle that. *I think I'll keep that little bit of information to myself for now. I don't need Norman freaking out.*

They both had a moment to think about the fact that they were on the same page. Then, Frank rolled over on his bed and said, "Norman, we keep all of this between just the two of us."

"I know, Frank."

"We can't let on to any of them that we're getting better."

Norman waved his hand in the air. "Don't you think I already know that?"

Frank was just making sure. "I just want to make sure we have all our ducks in a row before we attempt anything."

"I want to get out of this hellhole just as bad as you do, Frank. I won't slip up."

●

Every day, Norman and Frank took turns getting out of their hospital beds, stretching and walking around the room while the other one kept guard, listening at the door. They found they were getting much stronger and more capable of actually escaping.

One day, Frank was sitting up on the edge of his bed and wasn't paying attention to the door as he should have been. Norman was walking around in circles when the door opened.

Cassie stood in the doorway, shaken by what she saw. She gasped. "H-How long have you two been able to get out of your beds?" She didn't shut the door completely and the room had a little more light than usual.

Frank remained right where he was while Norman retreated and sat down on the side of his bed. Norman didn't say a word. He bowed his head and let Frank do all the talking. "I've been feeling better for about two weeks, Cassie. Norman's been improving for the last week or so. We didn't want you to know."

"Why not? Why wouldn't you let me know this was happening?"

"Why would we? After all, you're the one who's been trying to keep us sick, giving us all those injections and feeding us through tubes when we're asleep."

Cassie was stunned at Frank's words. She couldn't keep the angry tone out of her voice when she said, "No, Frank. That's not why I'm here. You got it all wrong, very wrong."

Frank sat back on his bed and crossed his arms. "Then, why don't you explain it to us, Cassie. My ears are burning."

"I wasn't hired to keep you sick. I was hired to make you well."

"Then why were you injecting the two of us with blood?"

Norman's eyes opened wide. He shouted, "Blood? What the fuck?"

"Yes, Norman. I didn't want to tell you that she's been putting foreign blood in us. I was afraid of how you'd react."

Norman sprang up off his bed and shouted, "How I'd react? How I'd fucking react? You knew and didn't tell me! Surely you didn't think I'd say, thank you ma'am, may I please have more fucking blood. How would anyone react when they find out

this bitch is injecting them with blood? What the
hell, Frank! I trusted you, man. You were all I had
left to believe in."

Frank understood. Norman was frightened
and he was angry. He'd made Norman feel that he
was in on their secret, a partner, only to find out that
Frank had not really trusted him at all, leaving out
the information about the blood.

Norman stood there, beating his fist against
his hand, looking first at Frank and then at Cassie.
He was becoming visibly more agitated as every
moment passed. She saw that Norman was totally
overwhelmed and could be a potential threat to her.
She took a small beeper from her jacket pocket and
pressed the button.

Frank inquired, "What did you just do with
that beeper?"

She stood there calmly, removed her mask
and said, "I called for backup."

"Backup?"

"Yes, backup. Norman's getting a little loud
and I don't know what he'll do."

Norman flitted his hand in the air. "Oh shit,
Cassie, I'm not going to do anything … as long as
you tell us what the hell is going on in this fucking
prison."

Then, Cassie backed away from Norman
and moved closer to Frank. She knew, of the two,
Frank was the one with the cool head. "Don't you

get it? I had to call for the others to come. That's our protocol when an employee feels they're in any kind of danger."

Frank calmly asked, "Do you really feel that you're in danger, Cassie?"

She stated, "Yes, a little. I mean, Norman was just shouting at me and hitting his fist. Just look at him."

"I was shouting at you because I just found out you've been sticking needles in us that were filled with someone or something else's freaking blood. That's why I was shouting, Cassie. That's why I was hitting my fist. I think that's a normal reaction."

Just then, Glenn and Wayne came into the room and saw Norman and Frank sitting up on the edges of their beds. Glenn asked, "What's going on in here, Cassie?"

Frank observed that none of them were wearing masks anymore. Cassie quickly walked across the room and stood with the orderlies. "We have a problem. They've both been getting better but never bothered to tell me."

Glenn asked, "How long has this been going on, Frank? Norman?"

Frank answered, "Does it matter? The point is that we're well enough to leave here now. There's no need to keep us anymore."

Norman chimed in. "Yeah, can't you see that we're fine?"

Cassie turned to Glenn and Wayne. They whispered back and forth to each other until Frank said, "Hey! Cut the shit! Me and Norman want to hear what you're talking about."

Cassie stopped whispering. She walked over to Frank and said, "This has all just moved up to the next level."

"What does that mean?"

Cassie lowered her head. "I'm afraid the time has come for me to back away from this situation. It's now time for our leader to come in and explain everything to the both of you. He is the authority and can enlighten you on matters that nobody else is allowed to explain."

"Your leader?"

"Yes, he's already been notified and will be here in a few minutes."

Frank and Norman stared at each other for a moment. They were even more confused than they had been before. Norman leaned on his bed, crossed his arms and inquired, "And after we meet with this guy, will we get out of here?"

"That's up to you, Norman."

Norman was tired of her riddles and never getting a straight answer. "What the hell does that mean, Cassie? How is it up to me? I've never been given a choice of what happens to me in here. Why should today be any different?"

Cassie cautiously approached Norman, put her hands on top of his hands and said in a gentle tone, "Just give him a chance to explain what's really going on here. I promise you, it's not what you think."

Norman gazed into her stunning hazel eyes and melted. He agreed to her wish with a nod of his head. He realized, without her mask on, she was beautiful and had an affectionate smile. "You know, Cassie, you're a real pretty woman, both inside and out."

"Thank you, Norman." She turned and began to walk away. "I guess I'll be seeing you around." She turned back to Frank and said, "See you, Frank. Good luck."

Glenn, Wayne and Cassie walked out of the room. Frank and Norman sat there quietly for a few minutes and waited. Impatience elevated Norman's temper again as he lashed out at Frank. Accusingly, he demanded, "I want to know how come you never told me about the blood, Frank." *Would you shut up about the goddam blood already?*

Frank mentally rolled his eyes. He knew Norman was going to make the blood thing bigger than it really was. He tried to defend his actions. "Cassie told me about the blood when I still wasn't sure if I could trust you, Norman. Now, what was I supposed to do? It was a bad choice."

"You could have taken a leap of faith and told me they were injecting me with blood. That's what you could have done. You don't start a new friendship with deceit."

"Well, I'm truly sorry. Now I realize that I should have trusted you."

Both men sat in silence for a few moments, staring away from each other while pondering their bizarre situation.

"She also told me about her race. She said she was a part of a dying race. I still have no clue what she meant by that."

Norman shrugged his shoulders and cast a baleful glance at Frank. "Get out of here. Doesn't make any sense to me either. But then again, I couldn't even be trusted with that bit of info, could I?" In response, Frank literally rolled his eyes. *How did I inherit this hot head?*

Norman glared at the door and asked, "How long are we just going to sit here and wait around for this bozo anyway? I thought she said he was on his way."

Just then, a man appeared in the doorway. He was a tall man with long blonde hair that was pulled back into a ponytail.

Rochelle, the nurse, was standing alongside him. Like the others, she was wearing no mask. She was spectacular. Both men stared at her dark empty eyes and her Mediterranean skin. She bowed her head to the blonde man and then stepped back into the hallway and left.

As the imposing man stepped through the door, Frank and Norman saw that his eyes were a brilliant golden yellow.

Frank knew those golden eyes. They were the eyes of the man in his dreams. Norman also knew those eyes from his dreams. Dreams that he and Frank had never discussed with each other. In fact, both men had experienced some of the same dreams, the garden, the speakeasy, the castle, the coffin people …

Their personal reactions to the dreams were different, of course, Frank's being somewhat more deductive and insightful than Norman's. They were two very different men.

The man entered the room and walked with a refined elegance. He wasn't dressed in scrubs like the others. No. He wore fashionable black trousers and a crimson silk shirt. There were big gold rings on several of his long, bony fingers, and in his ears were golden studs that glistened like gems. There was a pallor to his skin, not unpleasant but certainly noticeable. Courteously, he said, "Good evening, gentlemen. I see that you are both doing well." His voice was deep and mellow.

Frank looked over at Norman and asserted, "Let me do the talking this time." Norman nodded in agreement.

Frank approached the finely dressed man and said, "Cassie, our nurse, told us that you'd be able to explain everything to us."

"Of course, I will, my son. She did not have the authorization to do that because Cassie is only a level two employee. Only myself and the level fives have that type of clearance."

"Okay. Who are you?"

The man gave a quick laugh. "Oh, how rude of me. I do apologize. I never bothered to introduce myself. I am Tariq."

"What is this place?"

"This is a simple three-story warehouse that I have turned into a mini hospital. Well, not quite a hospital. It is more of a scientific facility." *Scientific facility? I knew it.*

"Why me? Why Norman?"

"Why not you? Frank, you were in that little bar, The Twisted Tail, at the right time. Norman was in another bar in Collinsville at the right time too. I own those bars and the motel and most every business in this town."

Norman was stunned. "Wow, you own the whole town?"

Tariq ignored Norman's comment and went back to the conversation with Frank. "I arranged for that little hit and run accident on the road. The man was an acolyte, if you will, who required discipline. Such an accident usually induces the driver to pull their vehicle into the next exit, which is Collinsville, and check into my motel. It's how we find new subjects."

"You said 'right time.' There is no 'right time' to be in your dumpy little bar, and the drinks were lousy too! Oh, and by the way, that motel wasn't exactly quality digs either. It could use some renovating."

Tariq chuckled gently and nodded his head. "It depends on whose perspective we're talking about, Frank. But since you so kindly reviewed my establishments, I'll certainly consider making some improvements."

Frank was starting to feel frustrated. "Why are we being injected with blood? Were you trying to kill us?"

Tariq began to laugh loudly. "Good heavens no. I was not trying to kill either of you. You were already dead and then I saved you."

Frank began to feel strangely uncomfortable with Tariq's words. "Already dead? But I didn't die. I think I'd know it if I was dead."

The man said sternly, "Oh yes, my son, you were dead, Frank. So was Norman. The poison that was added to your mixed drinks took care of that. But rest assured, you felt no pain."

"You poisoned us?"

"I certainly did. Poison is the quickest and most painless way to go. Indeed, I am the one who had the two of you murdered and then I brought you back to life."

"I beg to differ with you, Tariq. There was a lot of pain," Frank said.

"The pain you experienced was associated with bringing you back to life. But, your deaths, no pain." Tariq shrugged his shoulders, minimizing the agony he had inflicted.

Norman decided to add his two cents. He pointed his shaking finger at Tariq. "Impossible! If you had poisoned me and Frank, we wouldn't be standing here right now. I personally think you're full of shit."

Tariq seemed to graciously take Norman's rudeness in stride. He put his hands out and said, "There is much I have to explain to you. Please let me start from the beginning."

Finally, Frank and Norman were going to know what was going on. They gave Tariq their full attention. Norman said, "Alright, spill."

"I am the master of another race, a race that is very different from yours. It's a race that has been here since the dawn of time."

Frank questioned, "What race are we talking about here?"

"We are a race that survives on the blood of all living creatures."

Norman leaped up and shouted, "Vampires? There's no such thing!"

Tariq nodded his head and said patiently, "I can assure you, Norman, we are real. The vampire worlds that you read about in your books or that you watch on the silver screen are loosely based on our factual truth. We have been around forever, since the dawn of time."

Frank tried to remain calm, unlike Norman who kept flying off the handle. "That's a pretty big pill to swallow. How do we know if you're telling us the truth?"

Tariq smiled indulgently and spoke slowly, as if to calm Norman down. "I suppose the two of you would be the perfect example of the truth. Since you have been in captivity, tell me how much food have you consumed?"

Frank thought about it for a moment and then replied, "None, that I know of. I just assumed we were being fed with tubes when we were under sedation."

"You were not being fed while you slept. You haven't eaten anything since we took you four weeks ago."

"I've been gone for four weeks?"

"Yes, and Norman has been with us for nearly six weeks."

"You have been living, surviving on blood. To clarify more fully, you have been injected with my blood."

Frank paced around in a circle, staring at the tile floor, trying to absorb the ludicrous things that the eccentric man was telling him. "Does that mean that Cassie and the others are …?"

"Yes. Cassie has been with us for almost forty years now. She became a vampire when she was just a mere twenty-five."

Norman counted on his fingers. "That would make her sixty-five years old."

"That is correct, Norman."

Frank wanted to know. "Why? Why did you do this to us?"

Tariq understood why Frank and Norman were skeptical and continued patiently on with his story. He'd had to explain this story many times over with each new entry. "We did it because, like I said, we are a dying race. Between mishaps with the sunlight and the vampire hunters, our people have been dying off slowly for the last three hundred and fifty years. This was the only way we could find to repopulate, increase our numbers."

"And what about all the pain that we went through in here?"

Tariq demonstrated his sympathy with a nod of acknowledgement of their suffering, but subtly shrugged his shoulders at the same time. He looked at them with shrewd golden eyes and clarified, "The pain you felt was necessary. It was my blood that was preparing you to become a vampire. The pain in your throat, your stomach and your weakness. It was all part of your human body finally letting go of your old biology while your new vampire biology was taking over."

A niggling kernel of recognition tugged at Frank's subconscious even as he expressed his profound skepticism for the story. "Then, I'm a vampire? You're telling me that I'm a vampire and that blood sucking vampires really do exist in this day and age?"

"Yes."

"And Norman?"

"Norman is too."

"But I don't have fangs or sleep in a coffin and I don't crave blood."

Tariq beckoned them both out of their room. He guided them down the hallway to a small private room with two chairs and a sofa where they could sit down in comfort to finish their conversation. He told them, "You do not have a set of fangs that you can see or feel at the moment. Your vampire fangs will only extend out when you are feeding, and they will retract when you are finished."

"And what about the sunlight?"

"We cannot be exposed to sunlight for any great length of time. However, the artificial lights do not seem to bother our kind."

"And sleeping in the coffins? I saw coffin people in my dreams." Norman looked at Frank in surprise.

Tariq let out a quick chuckle. "It is 2021, Frank. Who needs to sleep in a constricted wooden box anymore when the world has created blackout curtains for us? It was as if the manufacturer had the vampire in mind."

"Why don't I crave blood?"

"Because you have been injected with the purest vampire blood on earth. That will satisfy your cravings for a time. My blood infused with a human blood is the only way to successfully create a powerful vampire. But regrettably, it has been a trial-and-error process."

Curiously, Frank inquired, "What do you mean by trial and error?"

Tariq shook his head sorrowfully, "Some of our patients have not been strong enough to get well with the infusions. Sadly, many have not survived the procedure. We've researched those numbers for years. On average, ninety percent of our patients have a fatal allergic reaction to the concentration of my blood. No matter. I am glad to see that the two of you are well."

Frank didn't know if Tariq was telling the truth or if he really was just some crazed cult leader who was out of his psychotropic meds. He wanted to get away from there. "Now that you've told us all of this, can we please leave?"

For the first time in their discussion, Tariq felt a bit of alarm. "It is not wise for you to leave our facility just yet. There is much for you to learn about the vampire laws and the history of how we came to be … how I came to be."

Norman groaned, "History?"

"Yes, Norman. The vampires have been here as long as humans have. You see, my child, what the Bible and the history books haven't told you is that Eve had another son. I was the first-born son of Eve, before Cain or Abel or Seth. I know that your dreams have revealed to you that Adam was not my father. I must tell you. This is true."

"Why isn't your name ever mentioned in the book?"

"I was actually the original sin. Eve's lust for my real father was what infuriated God and that is why they were punished with endless darkness. I was born at night, and for very many years after my birth, the sun did not rise in the sky. Night covered the earth for more than six years. My name, Tariq, means "night visitor.""

"Punished?"

"Adam and my mother realized that there was something wrong when I was a very young boy. At a very young age, I began to develop a hunger for blood. I would feed upon small animals. My parents were afraid of what I would eventually be capable of. By the time I was six, Adam decided that he had to remove me from their land. Toss me aside like garbage."

"How do you remove a six-year-old?"

"One very dark day, Adam took me and dragged me away. I did not want to leave my home but he was much stronger than I was. I remember, we walked for hours until we reached the Euphrates River. He picked me up and, with all his strength, thrust me into the raging water, hoping he would drown me. He showed no emotions or remorse that he was intentionally trying to murder me. I was a threat to him, you see."

Frank sat quietly as Tariq told his story, a story that Frank and Norman had already seen in their dreams. Frank observed his face and golden eyes. In spite of himself, Norman was enthralled. "What happened after that?"

"That was when I learned it is impossible to drown a vampire. Remember this fact, my children, as it could indeed save your lives. It has saved my life many times over the years."

Tariq watched Frank and Norman closely, scrutinizing their facial expressions and their body language, as he continued with his story. "I did not have the strength to stay afloat and I became so weak from not feeding that I sank into the water. I was just a small boy and I was terrified." Tariq paused his story as if he was in deep remembrance of that terror.

Then, he resumed. "As I was about to fill my lungs with the deadly water that would surely drown me, I found that I did not have to breathe. Breathing was wonderfully suspended while I was under the water. I drifted underwater a lot, mostly during the day, to avoid the sporadic sunlight because it was uncomfortable on my sensitive skin. I was perfectly content being submerged with the fish and other creatures of the water." Frank and Norman were listening intently. Tariq had told this story to many of his young vampires throughout the years.

"I swam for several days down the long and wild river until I was able to get to dry land that looked hospitable to me. The morning skies and the evening skies had finally returned to their normal cycles. As I had begun to understand while I was in the river, I learned quickly that I had to protect my flesh from the sun. Eventually, I wandered hundreds of miles and made a home where I could feed on the larger animals."

"I never saw my father, my mother or Adam again. I do not blame Adam and Eve though. They did not know what I was, and neither did I. But that is the story that is not in your edited version of the Bible. Indeed, my story was erased from its pages thousands of years ago."

"Erased?" Frank questioned.

"Yes, erased. The Bible is filled with lies. Lies flood its pages. Lies that its translators put in there to oppress. I have been there for many of the events that have taken place, and let me just say, the facts in that book are not always as accurate as they should be."

Frank and Norman were quiet. His story sounded real, but how could any of it be real? Or was it all fantasy, delusions of a mad man with a cult following.

Tariq stared at the wall. Theatrically, his eyes glazed with tears as he reflected on his juvenile years. The early events had been heart-breaking and traumatic but he had survived all of them and they had managed to give him the strength to carry on. "I hope I have explained myself well."

Frank knew there was a lot more that Tariq wanted to tell them, but he wanted Tariq to finish what he had to say so they could get out of there. *Jesus Christ, this guy is really long-winded.* "I'm really sorry about what happened, Tariq. But you mentioned something about vampire laws? What the hell are vampire laws?"

Tariq cleared his throat. "I have already told you about avoiding the sunlight and the effect it will have on you. About an hour before sunrise, you will begin to experience dangerous exhaustion and have great fatigue."

"Why is that?"

"Because, as I have said, the sunlight is our enemy. It is our leading cause of death amongst the vampire realm."

"Is there anything else?"

"Yes, Frank. There's a great deal more that you will need to know in order to survive out there in the darkness."

Frank crossed his arms and let out a long breath. "Okay. Let's have it."

Tariq could sense that Frank and Norman didn't care nearly as much about the warnings as they cared about leaving the facility. "What I have not told the two of you is how your bloodthirstiness will become insatiable if you do not feed regularly. Failing to nourish on the blood of living creatures, human beings, will progressively weaken you, make you hallucinate and will eventually cause you to disintegrate into ash."

Frank couldn't believe what he was hearing. He shook his head in disbelief when he said, "Okay, okay. Is that everything we need to know? Can we go now?"

Still not finished with his warnings, Tariq continued, "Any vampire can be hurt or paralyzed when splashed with holy water, or by the presence of a cross or the Bible."

"Paralyzed?"

"Yes, paralyzed, stunned."

"Our kind can be killed with a wooden stake driven through the heart, direct contact to silver, the sunlight, or by not feeding on blood for long periods of time."

Frank tapped his foot nervously. He was no longer concerned with anything Tariq was telling him. He wanted to go. *Come on, come on, old man. I've had enough.* "Is there anything else before we get the hell out of here?"

"Yes. You must be aware that, just as there are vampires, there are also vampire hunters. They are a brilliant and cunning group but their numbers have diminished like ours. If one of them discovers you, they will destroy you. Trust me, they are more callous than the vampires themselves. You must be very careful."

Frank realized he was still wearing the ugly light green scrubs that had been his uniform while he had been in the facility. Norman was wearing the same. He inquired, "Do you think it's possible for us to get some new clothes so we're not so obvious when we leave here?"

Tariq was now very concerned with Frank's attitude. He knew Norman would follow Frank's lead. Tariq said, "I wish you would think about this, Frank. I would rather you stay here for just a little while longer."

"Why? Why do you want us here? I said we're feeling good enough to go."

"I want to be sure that you can deal with the gift you have been given."

Norman spouted, "Gift? Go to hell, you sick bastard. We're leaving."

Tariq studied the two men thoughtfully for several moments. They represented success. They were in the ten percent of humans who had survived the ordeal. They were strong specimens that would make strong vampires.

However, he could easily make many more vampires if he wanted. All he needed was time and opportunity. These two had shown him disrespect and he did not like that. He made the decision. He would teach them a lesson. He would let them go to sink or swim in their new world. He chuckled to himself at his little joke.

Tariq pulled a cellphone from out of his shirt pocket and hit the green call button. "Yes. Could you please send down some clean clothes for Frank and Norman? Yes. They have chosen to leave us at this time. Thank you. I will let them know." He ended his call and informed the men that clothing, shoes, cellphones and some spending money were on the way.

Wayne arrived shortly thereafter with shirts, pants, shoes and wallets filled with money. Norman opened his wallet and said, "Holy shit, there's over a thousand dollars in here."

Tariq nodded graciously as though Norman had thanked him. He said, "Money is no object in the case of my children. I am a very wealthy man. I have been collecting my fortune for thousands of years. I am giving you these wallets with a little cash to help you begin your new lives as vampires. Your phones have a saved number in them, just in case you need to reach me."

The men got dressed as Tariq stood and watched them. Frank saw that he was ogling them and deriving pleasure from seeing them naked. He asked, "Is there something that you want to say to me, Tariq?"

Of the two men, Frank obviously had more potential and it was a shame that he was so rash and impatient. In spite of Frank's disrespectful behavior, Tariq liked him very much and hoped that he would survive his new life.

Tariq crossed his arms and grinned at Frank. "I was just wondering if you actually enjoyed the massage that I gave to you in that basement or were you just pretending to like it? I found that I enjoyed the touch of your warm flesh very much. But then you bit my hand. That was a very naughty thing to do, Frank."

Shocked and angry, Frank walked up to him and questioned, "That was you?"

Tariq smiled widely and proudly admitted, "The one and only."

"If you were in that basement with me, then you should know what happened to those other two people, Karen and Eddie."

"Oh them. I paid Eddie to poison you and then I poisoned him. Eddie did not fare as well as you did. The injections seemed to kill him quickly, made all of his internal organs swell up until they eventually ruptured. He made quite a mess for the men to clean up. As I said, it has all been trial and error. I have never seen any human who was that allergic to my blood. Oh well, he was no loss to the vampire world anyway."

"And Karen?"

"That girl was not poisoned. I only brought enough of the poison for you and that silly little bartender. She was not supposed to be there. I had to knock her out and put her in the basement until I could determine what to do with her. I injected her with tranquillizers to shut her up. I had planned to poison her here at the facility but, unfortunately, she managed to escape. She certainly is quite the sly little fox. The day that we were going to transport the two of you here, she just happened to find a way to slip past us."

Relieved to learn that Karen wasn't dead, Frank looked up at the ceiling and let out a lengthy breath. "Oh, thank God. She got away from you and she didn't die."

Tariq would say or do nothing more to stop Frank or Norman from leaving. He bowed his head and graciously shook their hands. "I wish you well, my children."

Frank and Norman weren't actually able to absorb everything that Tariq had told them. They still believed, they wanted to believe, that he was an insane underground cult leader who was living in some kind of fantasy world. All they longed for was their freedom.

Tariq tried to warn them again. "If you are wise, you will remember the instructions I gave to you. What I have told you will make it easier for you to exist in this new world. Heed my warnings. They are important. There is a car waiting for you at the main gate."

As they were leaving the room, Frank turned back and said, "I have one more question for you, Tariq. Why go through all this poisoning and blood injecting when you could just procreate? You know, have sex and get the woman pregnant. Or can't you do that anymore?" Frank looked at Tariq in mock innocence.

Tariq threw back his head and snickered. "Good one, Frank. That is a fair question. I certainly can have sex. As a matter of fact, all vampires enjoy sex on a far more heightened level than humans do. The pleasure is exquisite. However, I am so ancient that my seed is no longer potent -- but my blood is. All those who were born through the natural process have died out, except for me. All the others who are currently on this earth have died like you to become a vampire. I can resurrect the body with my blood, but not the seed. This process that you and Norman have survived leaves you with the ability to enjoy amazing sex but without the ability to produce life in the human way. I do hope this will not unduly distress you." Tariq continued to smile as he looked at Frank and Norman.

Frank was ready to get out of that jail cell he'd been in for weeks. He was feeling reckless. On the verge of freedom and more acutely aware of his surroundings, Frank asked bluntly, "And just where the hell are we anyway?"

Tariq explained, "You are only fifteen miles south of the town of Collinsville and the interstate is just a short distance from here."

Frank smiled and nodded and, just like that, both of them walked out. Tariq felt miserable that they'd left so suddenly after finding out the truth about what they had become. He wished that one of them, namely Frank, would change his mind, turn around and come back to the room. "Oh, Frank, why? Why?"

As they walked through the front doors and outside the building, Frank saw that it was evening. They got into the car, with a full tank of gas, and drove away from the facility.

CHAPTER THREE

As Frank drove north up the interstate and well over the speed limit, there was a long period of silent relief between him and Norman. He knew that they both had a lot to absorb and contemplate. What if they actually were vampires? Frank finally broke the silence and asked, "So, what do you think about what that guy had to say?"

"Personally, I think he was nuts … too many drugs as a teenager."

Frank nodded in relief that they were on the same page. "I think you're right. All those things he said just can't be true." *Can they?*

"So, what's the game plan, Frank? Where do we go now?"

"I want to get as far away from Collinsville and the land of crazies as possible. I was thinking we could make our way back to Harrisburg, clear our heads."

"Harrisburg? What's in Harrisburg?"

"That's where I live. We could take a little break from all this. Then, I can drive you back to …

wherever you're from. That's right. You never told me where you're from."

"I live in New Haven. That's in Connecticut. I lived there my whole life."

"Okay. We'll stop in Harrisburg and take a breather. Then I'll drive you back to New Haven. I can keep going to Boston."

"What's in Boston?"

"My sister, Marjorie and her husband and their kids. Marjorie must be worried sick about me. She's a level headed woman. Maybe she can help me make sense of this whole mess." *I need someone to make sense of it.*

"And you're just going to dump me off in New Haven and go?"

"Isn't that what you want? Don't you want to get home to see your family?"

Norman fixed his gaze on the horizon. Then he bowed his head regretfully while he spoke in a subdued voice. "I don't have any family, Frank. My mother and father died a long time ago. I never had any brothers or sisters. I never got married. I don't have kids and I work nine to five in a factory six days a week. Funny, I can't even tell you any of my coworkers' first names. I'm on my own. I have been for a long time."

Frank felt bad for Norman. It wasn't the first time he counted himself lucky he had Marjorie in his life. "I'm really sorry to hear all that, Norman. Sounds like you need a friend."

"Even though I've been gone for over six weeks, there wasn't anyone there who would miss me. If I disappeared tomorrow, no one would even notice. Then, I finally decided to let loose and take a week's vacation."

"Where was that?"

"Well, I was heading to New Orleans but I made the stupid mistake of stopping Collinsville for the night. I went out to a corner bar just on the edge of town and that's where they got me. I can't even take a vacation without something happening. It's just my luck."

Hearing Norman's history brought Frank's mood down. He wanted to show him some kind of compassion. "Well, Norman, it's not like you're alone anymore. After what we've been through together, I think you have a friend for life. You're the brother I never had."

With a glimmer of hopefulness in his eyes, Norman asked, "Really, Frank? Are we going to stay friends?"

Frank smiled and nodded. "Of course, we are. Remember, I'm the one who said I was taking you with me when I got out of that place. And you didn't think we could do it."

"You're right, Frank. I didn't believe you and I'm sorry about that. I was so miserable and I thought that you were just jerking my chain. I guess I felt like you were going to turn out to be one more disappointment in my life."

"Well, that's all behind us now. We got out of there together and we're going to stay together. You'll love my sister." They were both feeling a little embarrassed, so Frank punched Norman in the arm and Norman acted like it really hurt. The mood was lifted. *I like Norman better when he's not being such an asshole. If he was like this all the time, we might actually become friends.*

Frank and Norman continued to travel up the interstate throughout the night until five-thirty rolled around. That's when Norman asked, "Where are we now?"

"I think we're coming up on Winchester, Virginia. The last sign said that it should be about twenty miles ahead."

Norman's head dropped down sluggishly. "Suddenly, I'm not feeling so good."

Frank realized that he too was beginning to feel overwhelmed with exhaustion. "I know what you mean, Norman."

"What do you think it is? Could they have poisoned us again?"

Frank turned on the radio and waited to hear the announcer say the time. He heard the voice say that it was five-thirty in the morning. *Get the hell out of here. This is exactly what that old man said would happen.*

Frank knew they only had another hour until the sunrise. "I think we'd better pull over and get a motel room, just to be safe. We can sleep it off."

"Is this what Tariq was warning us about? I didn't feel this way until just now, an hour before the sun comes up."

Frank felt a tinge of worry, but he didn't want Norman to worry. "I don't think so, but just in case, we better stop at the first motel we see." *What if it's true?*

Twenty minutes later, Frank pulled the car into the Shady Rest Motel, just off the Winchester exit. Both men felt the fatigue growing rapidly. It was then that they both began to believe what Tariq had warned them about. *I know that I'm feeling it. I'm sure Norman is feeling even worse. I wish I knew if it was real.*

Frank stopped the car, walked up to the front desk, booked the room and paid for it in advance with cash. Then, both he and Norman, with as much speed as they could muster, entered the room and made sure that every curtain was closed completely, not allowing even a tiny drop of sunshine to find them there. *Just in case, we should do what Tariq said and avoid the sunlight.*

Within minutes, Frank and Norman had put a "Do Not Disturb" sign on the door, gotten out of their clothes and into their separate beds. They had both fallen into a deep and soothing sleep that lasted through the day.

•

That evening, Frank rolled over and looked at the bright red numbers on the nightstand clock. He saw that it was eight o'clock at night. He turned around to tell Norman the time but Norman's bed was empty. Wait! Norman was lying next to him in his bed.

He shook him. "Norman, wake up. It's eight o'clock. We have to get going."

Norman opened his eyes. He felt awake and alive. He hadn't felt so much energy since he was a kid. He sat up and asked, "What am I doing in this bed, Frank?"

"I don't know. I thought you might be able to tell me."

Norman cocked his head and tried to retrace everything from the past fourteen hours. "I know I was in that bed when I went to sleep. I did have a strange dream though."

Frank began to recall a strange dream of his own. "Tell me, what exactly did you dream about, Norman?"

Norman was embarrassed to say. "I think we should just let it go, Frank."

Frank insisted. "No, Norman. I don't want to let it go. Tell me. Please."

He struggled to tell Frank about the dream. "I dreamt that I got out of my bed and got into your bed. You opened your eyes and extended your hand to me, inviting me in."

Norman paused and Frank waited. "Is there more, Norman?"

"I'm pretty sure, Frank."

Frank waited to hear it. "You'd better spit it out then, Norman."

Picking up a head of steam as he began to recount the dream, Norman continued. "Well, then we kissed and then it went further. It went a lot further, Frank."

"Hold on, Norman. Stop making shit up and stop joking."

"It's no joke, Frank! Listen to me! You did take it one step further!"

"Stop it! I did not!"

"Yes, you did. I know because I felt your teeth scrape me a little."

"That's enough, Norman. I don't want to hear any more about your fucked up wet dream. I wouldn't have brought you with me if I'd known you were into guys."

"Me? Into guys? What about you, Frank? You seemed to like it just fine."

"Shut the fuck up! I've hardly ever done the homo thing in my life."

Norman laughed. "Hardly ever? Well, I beg to differ with you this time, Frank. I know for a fact that you kissed me and went down on me." Frank had heard enough.

"Shut the fuck up!" Frank jumped out of the bed, circled it, and dragged Norman to the floor. He held him down and raised his fist threateningly over Norman's face.

As Frank was about to deliver a blow, he saw that Norman was smiling and deriving some erotic pleasure from their fight. For that matter, so was Frank.

Frank sprang up and sat on the bed. Norman got up and was about to join him. "Get on your own bed and stay there."

"Okay, Frank."

They sat on their separate beds for several minutes trying to wrap their minds around what they had done. They stared around at everything in the room with owlish interest, except each other. It was uncomfortable and a little disturbing to say the least.

As the situation became more ludicrous and unendurable, it became apparent that someone had to break the silence.

Frank broke first. He had to admit that he shared the same memories with Norman. "So ... I

… I …" Frank swallowed hard and said, "Now, I remember, everything that happened, Norman, and it wasn't a dream. It happened."

"I know."

"But it'll never happen again, never ever. I can tell you that."

Trying to go along with the program and explain the situation away, Norman said, "I hear you, Frank. I'm straight. I have been my whole life. I always liked girls. I don't know what in the world would possess me to do something like that? It's not my scene."

"I'm straight too, Norman, except for a time or two when I was in college."

Norman gave Frank a sour look. "A time or two in college?"

"I was experimenting. And besides, nothing ever came of it."

They continued to sit on their separate beds and ponder what they had done in that dark motel room. They didn't make eye contact. Frank didn't want to admit it, but he remembered the pleasure. He'd enjoyed his experience with Norman. *Why with Norman?*

And Norman was, strangely, not his usual cantankerous self. They both knew that what took place was something that was connected to the new vampire thing. But, compared to what had happened to them during their painful vampire transition, the shared sexual experience brought them comfort and a strange sense of fulfillment.

Then, out of nowhere, Norman asked, "Do you think my dick is bigger, Frank?"

Frank looked at Norman with astonishment painted all over his face. *What the hell is this guy talking about?* "How the hell would I know? Stop talking, Norman."

"Well, is yours?"

"Is my … what?"

"Is your dick bigger?" Norman just wouldn't let it drop.

"I don't know. And mine doesn't have to be bigger. Okay? There's never been a problem with my size. I know because all the ladies tell me so." Frank stared belligerently at Norman, challenging him to argue.

Norman stood up. "Alright, Frank. Let's get our shower."

"Our shower?"

"Yeah. It'll be faster if we both go in at the same time."

Frank contemplated for a moment. Then, he got up and went into the shower with Norman. And they did it all over again.

As they took their belongings and walked out of the motel together, Frank smiled at Norman. Encouraged, Norman smiled back.

"So, what do you think, Frank?"

"What do I think about what, Norman?"

"Is my dick bigger?"

Frank chuckled. "I swear to God, Norman, one more word about dick sizes and I'll drown you in the bathtub."

The men looked at each other and laughed together because they both knew that it's impossible to drown a vampire.

As Frank turned back onto the interstate, he said, "Next stop, Harrisburg."

Everything was okay between Norman and Frank but their conversations that night were few and far between as they both silently wondered if they were going to sleep in the same bed again. Momentary glances were exchanged but very few words were spoken.

At one point, as they were passing the exits for Hagerstown, Maryland, Norman noticed all the lit-up billboards for all the fast-food restaurants and realized, "You know, Frank, we still haven't eaten anything."

Frank agreed. "That's right, and I'm not even hungry. It is strange that Tariq said we didn't eat food anymore."

Norman confessed, "But I think he was right about something else."

"What's that, Norman?"

"I'm beginning to crave something else. It's what he said we needed."

"Blood?"

"I think so, Frank. I don't know why but the urge is getting stronger and stronger. I was a little hungry for it when I woke up, but now the thirst is getting overwhelming."

Frank glared at Norman and said, "I've been thinking the same thoughts. I can feel it too, but I'm not going to give in."

"You're not?"

"That would be insanity. I can't bite another person and suck the blood from their body. I could never kill another human being."

"Then we better figure something out soon. I don't know how much longer I can go on with these feelings."

"We're almost home. Let's just get there and we'll figure it out then."

"Okay, Frank. I didn't mean to sound like a crazy man. You know what's best. I'll just keep my mouth shut now."

●

Frank and Norman finally made it back to the house by one o'clock in the morning. Norman took a look around at the small house and remarked, "Nice place you got, Frank."

"Thanks, Norman."

"I guess you're not too far away from the downtown area."

He didn't know why Norman was asking him about the downtown. "No, it's just about ten blocks away, a hop, skip and a jump." *We'll worry about a grand tour of the city later. Right now, I need to relax and unwind.*

Frank wanted to make sure Norman had everything he needed to feel at home. He looked over at Norman and said, "I'd say that we're about the same height and weight. You're welcome to use whatever clothes I have in the closet. Mi casa es tu casa."

He pointed around the house at the different rooms. "That way is the bathroom. Over there is the bedroom. And the kitchen is that way. Do you have any questions?"

"Yes."

"What do you need to know?"

"Is there only one bedroom?" Norman didn't show it but he was hoping that Frank would say that it was the only one.

"I'm afraid so, bud. It's only a one bedroom, one bath." Frank hid the fact that he was excited the two of them would have to share a bed again. Frank put his hand on Norman's shoulder, rubbed it and said, "I say we get some shuteye."

Norman enjoyed that Frank was rubbing his shoulder. "I think I'm going to take a shower first. I stink. You know, we were in that hot car for almost four hours."

"Okay, you take a shower. I'm exhausted from the driving. I can hardly keep my eyes open. I'm going to sleep."

Norman smiled. "Okay, Frank. I'll be there in a couple of minutes."

Norman waited for a little while until Frank retreated to the bedroom. He didn't really want to shower. He was ravenous and he wanted blood. The hunger inside was overwhelming. It was all that he could think about.

Norman planned to sneak out of the house once Frank had fallen asleep. He was sure he could find someone in the streets of Harrisburg to end the aching starvation, the bloodlust that had begun to control his thoughts.

When he was sure he could leave the house without waking Frank, Norman slipped out the back door and walked quickly through the neighborhood. He could see everything clearly with his new night vision, as if it was daytime. Oh great, night vision. Just another perk of being a vampire, he thought balefully.

He walked across Bailey Street and then up North 14th Street. He saw no one in the sleepy little streets. He continued on down State Street until he eventually reached Front Street, the downtown of Harrisburg. "This is the place."

Norman saw that, by that hour, all the bars had already emptied out. He could feel the intense hunger that was growing ever stronger inside him. He searched everywhere he could. The restaurants were. The bars and nightclubs were closed, and the streets were empty. "Wow, this city has no nightlife at all."

Unexpectedly, he turned around and saw someone walking on a dirt path alongside the river. He realized this was the perfect opportunity. He could feed off them and then just throw them in the river. No one would ever discover the body. He walked towards the person, trying not to draw any attention to himself.

As Norman got closer, he saw that it was a woman and she was all by herself. He walked up behind her. She turned around and saw him but she didn't appear surprised.

Norman noticed her silky dark-red hair and gleaming green eyes. She inquired, "Are you here to drink my blood?"

Norman was dumbfounded. His fangs hadn't fully emerged yet. He knew that he didn't look like any of the vampires in the movies. "Why would you say that to me, miss?"

"Because I know who you are. I know what you are."

"How? How can you know that?"

She glared at him, then smiled and said, "I can smell a vampire from twenty yards away, and you are a vampire."

"I don't understand."

"Then allow me to introduce myself. My name is Karen."

"Karen?"

She stood there and looked into his eyes and waited for him to make the connection. Eventually, he realized she was the same Karen that Frank had told him about. "You're Karen? You're the woman from the dive bar?"

"That's me."

"You were the one who was locked in the same basement as Frank?"

"One in the same."

"Tariq said that you had escaped captivity. But why are you here in Harrisburg? Does Frank know you're here?"

"No, Frank doesn't know I'm here, not yet. I followed the two of you from the moment you left the facility."

As Norman spoke to her, he was distracted. All he could do was concentrate on her throat and her jugular vein. He could hear her heart beating as it was pumping blood through her body. He didn't care if she and Frank were almost bed buddies. He was starving and he had to have her, whatever the repercussions. He asked, "Why did you follow us here? Do you need protection?"

"No. I don't need protection. I'm the last person who needs protection. I know how to take care of myself."

"Then why are we standing here, Karen? I don't understand."

"Didn't Tariq even bother to warn you about the vampire hunters?"

Norman was beginning to tense up. "He did. He told us to beware of them, but I thought he was full of shit."

Karen stepped closer to Norman. Her breath got heavier. Norman's breath got more rapid. Then, she said, "I think you'd better start running. I'm the one he warned you about."

"You're a vampire hunter?"

"I am."

"Tariq was telling us the truth?"

"He was."

"The vampire hunters are real?"

"We are."

"The whole time Frank was locked in that fucking basement, being turned into a vampire, he was sharing the same space with the one who wants to destroy him?"

"That was just a fluke, a stupid mistake on my part. I was actually tracking Tariq but Eddie the bartender got in the way of my plan. And, when I finally woke up, Tariq had me down in that filthy basement too."

"You were going to kill Tariq?"

"Yes, he's our primary target. He's always been our main focus."

"Always?"

"Yes, Norman. I come from a long lineage of vampire hunters that dates back for more than five hundred years when my ancestors first found Tariq in Moldavia. He and his creations slaughtered my ancestors, and we have a very long memory. If we can get rid of him, then no more of your kind can ever be created. We know that his blood is the only blood that can create a vampire. It's our chance to end them."

Frightened, Norman started to back up from Karen, inch by inch. When he was a few feet away, he turned and started running back down the same streets that he'd come from. Norman knew that he needed to race back to the house and away from Karen. His new strength enabled him to run at an accelerated speed even while he was in the early stages of bloodlust.

But Karen chased after him. Her lifetime of training as a vampire hunter gave her the strength to almost match Norman's speed. She trailed behind but not by much. As they ran through the streets of Harrisburg, Norman saw that Karen was gradually catching up to him.

Once he was on Bailey Street, he found the house and ran towards it. Then, he raced to the back yard. By the time he reached the back door, Karen had caught up to him.

As she stood right next to him, out of breath, she smiled and said, "Thank you, Norman. You are truly the dumbest vampire I've ever met." She let out a chuckle.

"Why is that?"

"You're a real idiot. You just led me right to Frank's house. I'm going to destroy him right after I destroy you."

Just then, Norman shouted, "Frank, get out of here! It's Karen!"

Karen became angry and aggressive. "Shut up, Norman!"

Norman shouted louder. "The girl from the basement is a vampire hunter!"

"I said shut up, Norman!"

"She's going to kill me! Then, she's coming for you! Get out of here, Frank!"

Frank woke up from a dead sleep when he heard Norman shouting outside. He ran to the back door and saw Norman and Karen standing there. He heard Norman shout out again, "Frank! She's here to kill us! Get out!"

Then, Norman watched dumbly as Karen pulled a wooden stake from the pocket of her jacket and stabbed it into his chest. Norman screamed in shock and misery.

Frank watched in alarm as Norman's body began to combust internally. He saw smoke and flames pouring out from everywhere and soon there would be nothing but ashes on the ground where Norman had been.

Karen had to back up while the acrid fire and smoke consumed Norman's body from the inside out, flames spitting from every orifice. She spotted Frank looking out through the back door window. She knew she would have to move fast or she'd lose him.

He turned, grabbed his keys and a shirt and ran out the front door as fast as he could. He jumped into his car.

By the time Karen made her way around the house and to the driveway, Frank was speeding off into the night. She shook her head and said, "Well, at least I got one of them, the senseless one. Frank can't go far. I'll find him."

Karen took a phone from her jacket pocket and pushed the call button. She waited. "Yes, it's me. I got one of them but the second one got away. I may need some backup."

"We can't afford to send you any backup right now, Karen. You're going to have to handle this one on your own."

"No backup?"

The voice on the other end said, "It's one vampire. I think you're capable of handling a single vampire, a new one at that."

Karen exhaled a long breath and looked up at the night sky. "Okay, I'll do what I can, but this is bullshit, Dean."

"I'm truly sorry, Karen. You know that our numbers are low. The others are out on missions of their own. I can't spare anyone."

Karen realized there was nothing he could do to help and she knew it was going to be just her. "Alright then. I'll call you when I've finished the job, Dean."

"Good luck and God speed, Karen. I'll be waiting for your call."

Karen hung up from her call and looked up to the night sky again. A tear, borne of dread and maybe regret, rolled down her cheek.

Then, in an abrupt fit of rage and frustration, she dropped the phone on the ground and stomped on it over and over until it was broken into pieces. "Fuck you, Dean! Fuck you!"

●

Frank was filled with horror at what he'd seen, but he tried to tamp down his hysteria. *Don't think about it. Don't think about Norman. Focus on the road.*

Frank zipped up the interstate with the car pointed towards Boston. He wanted to feel safe and he knew there was only one person in the world that he trusted completely, his sister Marjorie. *Marjorie will help me figure this out.*

He looked at his watch and saw that the hour was late, two-thirty. He had to get as far away from his home in Harrisburg and Karen as he could. But he knew he'd never make it all the way to Marjorie before the sunrise.

Frank accelerated even faster until he was going ninety miles an hour, hoping he didn't get pulled over.

As he made his way through Pennsylvania, Frank checked his watch again. It was four-thirty in the morning. He knew he only had another hour to make it to safety.

Frank got as far as Danbury, Connecticut when he began to feel the fatigue that came hand in hand with the sunrise. He looked at his watch and saw that it was five-forty-five. He had to find some out-of-the-way motel.

He took the Danbury exit and drove until he saw a sign for the Happy Trails Motel. He pulled into the parking lot, walked into the building and told the front desk clerk that he needed a room for one day. Again, he paid in cash. *I can't have any kind of paper trail.*

In the room, Frank closed all the curtains to make sure that no sunlight peeked in. He sat on the side of the bed and took a moment to calm down and reflect on what had happened to Norman in Harrisburg.

Now, he knew that Karen was one of the vampire hunters that Tariq had warned him about. He wished he had been more appreciative and interested in the history that Tariq had offered while he was still in the facility. *Why didn't we take the time to listen to him?*

Was it finally time to call Marjorie and let her know that he was on his way? Should he tell her that he was a vampire? Should he tell her that he'd been dead for four weeks? *How will she react when I tell her the truth?*

Then he became furious when he thought about Norman again and how that bitch destroyed him. *That damned Karen! That bitch! That fucking vampire hunter!*

He found that he missed Norman more than he probably should have. But he appreciated that they had shared something special, something that was just between them.

Firstly, there was the fact that they were both murdered and transformed into blood-sucking vampires without their knowledge and against their will. Secondly, there was the passionate night they had spent together and the stimulating shower that took place afterwards. Then there was the yearning to spend another night together. *I wanted it as much as Norman did.*

"What do I do?" He looked around the room and said, "She'll never find me here and she has no idea where I'm going."

Frank felt safer believing that Karen was probably still searching for him in Harrisburg or the surrounding areas.

He glanced over at the alarm clock on the nightstand and saw that it was six-fifteen. He was hungry but couldn't do anything about it. The sun would be rising soon. Frank knew that the intense bloodthirst growing inside him was that same thirst that had driven Norman into the dark vacant streets of Harrisburg.

Frank felt extreme exhaustion creeping up quickly, mixed with the penetrating desire for the blood of a human victim. *I'm so hungry but I have to get some rest.*

Suddenly, he had an idea. He remembered that Tariq had given him the cellphone and had said to call him if he needed anything. What seemed like ages ago had been just a few hours. *Is this the way my life is going to be?*

Frank grabbed the phone and found the only number listed in it. He hit the call button and hoped Tariq would answer before he fell asleep. It rang several times but no one picked up on the other end. *What the hell, Tariq.*

Frank was determined to get an answer from the creature that had made him this way. He hit the call button again. It rang twice and then Frank heard his voice. "Frank?"

"Tariq. Thank God."

"This is a difficult time for a phone call. It is almost time for the sun to rise."

"I know what time it is, Tariq, but I need your help."

"You sound as if you are in trouble. What is the matter, my child?"

Nervously, Frank said, "Norman is dead. He was stabbed through the heart with a wooden stake by a vampire hunter."

Surprised, Tariq questioned, "How did the vampire hunter find him so quickly? Usually, their kind is not so fast."

"It was Karen."

"Who?"

"Karen."

"Who on earth is this Karen person?"

"She was the girl in Collinsville that was in that damned basement with me. She's one of them, a vampire hunter."

There was a brief moment of silence before Tariq deduced, "Well, she must have been there to destroy me. After all, I have been the main target of that group for hundreds of years. It is too bad that I have not been able to find the only five remaining in the group."

Frank yawned. "I'm starting to get tired. I need help from you."

"Anything for you, my son. What is it that you need exactly?"

"I need to get to my sister's house in Boston but I don't feel safe anymore. I don't know who's a vampire hunter out there."

Tariq could perceive that Frank was getting himself worked up. Even so, he felt a great need to deliver a stern lecture. "I want you to recall, Frank, that I tried to warn you, but you and Norman were too impatient to listen to me. I only wanted to make sure you remained safe."

"I know that now and I'm sorry, Tariq. I really am."

"Now, you are paying the consequences for your arrogance. Norman paid the ultimate price for his. But I am still willing to save you. I will send someone to come there and get you. Would you like that, my child?"

Frank didn't know how to answer him. He needed Tariq's help but he didn't want to be taken back to the facility. He wanted to get to Boston to see Marjorie. "I don't want you to come here and take me back. I need help to get to my sister. I need to be with her."

Again, Tariq was stern. "I see that you are still willing to make imprudent choices, Frank, but I cannot stop you. Where are you? Are you still there in Harrisburg?"

Frank was hesitant to give his whereabouts at first. He yawned again. He wasn't sure yet if he could trust Tariq. But then he recalled that Tariq was the one man who'd provided him and Norman with all the warnings they had foolishly chosen to ignore.

He took a leap of faith and told Tariq. "No, I'm not in Harrisburg anymore. I got my ass out of Pennsylvania and made it as far as Connecticut. I'm in Connecticut."

"Well, Frank, Connecticut covers a lot of miles. Could you be a little more specific? It will make my job much easier."

"I'm in Danbury."

"Are you at a motel?"

"Yes, I'm at the Happy Trails Motel. I'm in room 217. The place is a dump."

Tariq let out a small chuckle. "Why am I not surprised, Frank? Alright, someone will be there as soon as the sun sets."

There was a long period of silence and Tariq knew that Frank wanted to say more. Tariq hoped it was a thank you. "I think you should tell me what you want to say before the sunrise. We do not have much time left."

"My craving."

"What about your craving?"

"It's getting stronger. It's like, all I can think about is blood."

"I told you that would happen. It will only get worse if you don't feed. Eventually, as I said, it will become all-consuming until it finally ends your time on earth."

"You had told me that you fed on animals when you were a child. I saw you feeding on them in my dreams. Is that still possible for me? Can I get by on the blood of non-humans?"

"Certainly. I was forced to feed off animals for many years, but their blood does not provide the same power as the blood of humans. You would have to bite many of those miniscule little creatures to absorb the same strength that you would get from one human."

"I don't care how many animals I have to go through, as long as I don't have to murder humans. I won't do that!"

Frank heard Tariq laughing on the other end of the line. *Is he laughing at my misery?* "What's so funny, Tariq?"

"Almost every brand-new vampire believes that they can change the rules, change the way it has been for thousands of years."

"But it can be done?"

"Feeding on animals will only help to get you by but it will never catapult you to your full potential, your full strength. Remaining weak like that will only make you easier prey for the vampire hunters, my son."

"But what if I found a way to take the blood of a large animal? Won't that be the same as human blood?"

"The larger the animal, the better for you, but it is still not as nutritious to vampires as human blood. It will still leave you with the hunger. And where are you going to find an animal big enough to ease your cravings, at the local zoo?" Frank found it annoying that Tariq seemed to find his predicament amusing.

"I just don't think that I can murder another human being in cold blood, Tariq. I'm not designed that way."

Frank heard another chuckle from Tariq before he explained, "Actually, it is not cold blood. It is warm and delicious."

Frank wanted to be repulsed by what Tariq had said but knew that it was probably true, feeling he'd love to taste human blood.

Tariq said, "I am terribly sorry to hear about your new friend Norman but I do hope you enjoyed your time together before he was ended. I hope you spent your time wisely."

Tensely, Frank whispered, "I don't know what you mean."

"Yes, you do. You were placed in the same room with Norman because we knew you would be compatible as companions."

"Companions?" *Companions? Norman and me? Companions?*

"Let me explain something to you, Frank. In our world, we have no boundaries, no clear rules as to who should be with whom on a sexual or intimate level. As I told you, our sex life is vastly superior to the sex life of humans."

"I think I'm learning that."

"I have had many companions throughout my long lifetime. Male, female, it does not matter. Furthermore, we excel in the act and our "thirst" for sex, shall we say, is unparalleled. There is and never will be any judgement here, Frank. That is my gift to you."

Frank leaned down on the bed. His eyelids were getting heavier by the moment. Tariq knew the call was about to end. "I will make sure someone is there for you at the Happy Trails Motel just after the sun sets. Have a good sleep, Frank. I will pray that you are alright."

Frank could no longer keep his eyes open. He sensed that Tariq was feeling fatigued too. He lowered his head and mumbled, "Thanks for your help, Tariq."

The last thing that Frank did was hit the red button on the cellphone. Then, he collapsed lower down on the bed. He grabbed the soft pillow, put it under his head and fell into a deep and restful sleep where he dreamt of Norman. *Norman, why did you leave me?*

•

Frank was awakened at fifteen minutes after nine by a loud knocking on his motel room door. He jumped out of the bed and immediately wondered if Karen had somehow found him. *That's impossible. She could never find me here.*

He sat on the edge of the bed and remained silent and still as he waited. He could feel his hands trembling. He acknowledged that, if it was Karen or some other vampire hunter on the other side of that door, he had no protection and would probably have a wooden stake driven into his heart, just as she had done with Norman. *I better start carrying a gun or some kind of weapon.* His thoughts bounced around as he wondered if vampire hunters were immune to bullets. Frank had no knowledge of what they were capable of. He never waited around long enough to find out. *I'm such an idiot. I should've asked Tariq those questions.*

The knocking and banging soon turned into pounding. Then, Frank heard a voice coming from the other side of the door. "Frank, wake up. I've come to get you out of here."

The voice sounded almost familiar to Frank. He took a chance and peered cautiously through the peephole. It was Rochelle, only Rochelle. Frank let out a sigh of relief, opened the door and invited her in. "Are you alone?"

She stood in the doorway and replied, "Yes, Frank. It's just me."

"I wouldn't have guessed that Tariq would send you."

She said snappishly, "Why is that, Frank? Is it because I'm a woman?"

Frank became nervous and defensive. "No, that's not what I meant."

She demanded an answer. "Then, what did you mean?"

"It's just that you were always so quiet back at the facility."

She grinned. "Frank, haven't you ever heard that it's the quiet ones you have to watch out for? Don't forget, I'm the one your mother warned you about." She laughed a seductively evil laugh as she entered the motel room.

Rochelle was toting a large brown suitcase over her shoulder. She peered around at the room and saw it was truly a dump like Frank had told Tariq. She glared at him. "This is the best place you could find?"

He ignored the question and asked, "What's in the suitcase?"

Rochelle dropped the big suitcase at Frank's feet. "It's clean clothes. I figured that you could use them and maybe a shower after that vampire hunter probably made you shit your pants." Rochelle let out a giggle. She thought her joke was funny. Frank didn't.

He didn't bother to respond to Rochelle. He asked, "Did Tariq send you here alone? Why didn't he send Wayne or Glenn too?"

Rochelle leaned over as if there was a room full of people and she didn't want them to hear her. "Between you and me, Wayne and Glenn aren't cut out for what I do. Besides, they're still on level one, like you."

Frank still didn't know what level one, two or five meant but he nodded his head and smiled as if he understood anyway.

Rochelle continued to explain away Wayne and Glenn. "Those two do better when they stay back at the facility. And Wayne can get a little jittery sometimes. I, on the other hand, am one of Tariq's lead people in the field, level four. I've been working my way to level five."

Then, Frank was curious. "If vampires can't be exposed to the daylight, how did you get all the way here from Collinsville?"

"Tariq told you he was a very wealthy man with a great many toys at his disposal. I borrowed one of his helicopters and headed to Danbury when the sun went down."

Frank was in awe of the many things he was learning about the inner workings of the vampire world. In utter shock, he questioned, "You actually brought a fucking helicopter all the way to Danbury to help me?"

Rochelle answered, "I didn't fly it. One of our other field men gave me a ride and then went back to the facility."

"Wow. That's service."

"And I have a car waiting for us outside as soon as you're ready to go."

Frank wanted to make sure Rochelle was clear on the plan. "And you're going to take me to see my sister in Boston?"

"Those were the orders that I received from the boss, Frank."

Frank picked up the brown suitcase, opened it, and took out the clothes he'd need. Then, he said, "Well, thanks for the clothes, Rochelle. I promise I'll be quick with the shower."

Rochelle hinted, "Do you think you'll need any help in there?"

Frank stared at the beautiful curves of her body but tried his best to focus on the task at hand, not more sex. "I think I know how to take a shower on my own."

"Are you sure, Frank?"

"I'm okay, Rochelle."

Rochelle smiled at Frank and asked, "Well, can I come in and watch?"

Frank rolled his eyes. He finally grasped the fact that this new world was a very sexually driven world without inhibitions.

As he walked into the bathroom, he realized that he was just as driven as Rochelle. He turned to her and smiled, once again giving into the sensuous pleasures. "Sure, you can watch. I may need you to wash my back."

Like an excited child, finding all of her gifts beneath the tree on Christmas morning, Rochelle enthusiastically clapped his hands together, kicked off her shoes, unbuttoned her silky blouse and then swiftly followed Frank into the bathroom.

As he stood next to the shower, removing his clothing, he looked back and saw the beautiful olive-skinned Rochelle with dark and empty eyes, standing there, completely naked. Every part of her body was ready.

He was a bit embarrassed when he looked down and saw that he already had an erection. She liked what she saw.

He said, "You're naked, Rochelle."

"I didn't want to get my clothes wet when I was washing your back."

Frank leaned into the shower and spun the handle to turn on the water. Steam from the hot shower began to fill up the bathroom and Frank stepped into the shower.

Rochelle followed him into the comforting hot water and they remained in there for the next forty-five minutes.

•

As they approached the car, Rochelle put her hand up and announced, "I'll do the driving and you can rest."

Frank asked, "Why can't I drive?"

Rochelle spun the key chain and explained, "I want to get us there in one piece, Frank. We can't afford any accidents right now. Besides, I have this strange feeling you have a lead foot and you're very emotional right now. Anyway, haven't you learned anything from Tariq? The level ones don't make the rules. I do."

Frank couldn't argue with her. It seemed as if Rochelle knew his driving habits better than he knew himself. Unquestioningly, he shrugged his shoulders, walked to the passenger side and said, "I suppose you're right."

"Of course, I'm right."

They got into the car and headed towards the highway. Rochelle let Frank know, "If we maintain the speed limit, we should get into Boston between ten and eleven."

"Marjorie should still be up." *I hope and pray that she's still up.*

"Do you want to maybe call your sister to let her know that you're on your way, instead of us just showing up at her front door?"

"I suppose I should."

Rochelle handed Frank his phone. "There you go, Frank."

Frank dialed Marjorie's number and listened to the rings. "Hello?"

"Marjorie? Marjorie."

"Frank? Oh my God!"

"It's me."

"Oh, thank God! Is that really you, Frank?" He could hear the happiness and relief in the tone of her voice.

Rochelle could also detect the happiness in Frank's voice. "It's me."

"Are you okay?"

"I'm as good as I can be." *Aside from the fact that I was kidnapped, murdered and turned into a vampire.*

Now that she knew he was alright, the grief Marjorie had been feeling for a month began to turn to anger. "What's going on? Where have you been for the last four weeks and why didn't you bother to contact me?"

He didn't want to spill his guts to his sister over the phone, or in front of Rochelle. "Marjorie, you'd never believe it if I told you." *How do I even begin to explain this?*

She insisted. "Try me."

"I don't want to get into this right now, not over the phone. I'm on my way to Boston and we'll see you soon."

"You're coming to Boston?"

"Yep. We're still about two and a half hours away from you."

Marjorie paused. Then, she inquired, "You said 'we.' Who is 'we'?"

"I brought a friend along with me. Her name is Rochelle."

Rochelle leaned over and yelled towards the phone, "Hello, Marjorie! We'll see you in a little while!"

Uh-oh. That stern side of Marjorie was coming out and Frank was about to be mothered. "Frank, what's going on? First, you vanish from the face of the earth for a month, and now, you reappear and just decide to drive seven hours to Boston, in the middle of the night, and you're just happening to bring a friend, a woman friend. Is she what this is all about?"

Frank didn't want to do this. He wanted to be face to face with her when he broke the bizarre news to her. He had no idea how she would react. After all, her brother was actually dead and he was a vampire. "Marjorie, if you ask me to explain over the phone again, I'm going to hang up. Can we just not do this now?"

Uneasily, she yelled at him. "Okay! Okay! Have it your way!"

"Thanks, Marjorie."

She wasn't done. She continued. "All I can say is that this better be good. You had me and the kids thinking you were dead. I had to deal with calls from your boss, your neighbors, and all of those late bills that I had to take care of for you, coupled with the damned fact I thought I'd never see you again. Jesus Christ, Frank!"

Frank looked over at Rochelle. Rochelle saw the harassed and wild look in Frank's eyes. "Frank, are you alright?"

Frank mumbled to Marjorie. "Sis, I have to go now. I'll see you soon."

After Frank ended the call, he slid down in his seat and stared straight ahead. He was pale and his forehead was dripping sweat. Rochelle drove the car into a rest area and parked far back in a dark and isolated corner of the parking area. She knew what was wrong. She'd seen that look before in new and resistant vampires. "Are you fucking kidding me, Frank? You still haven't fed?"

Weakly and unsteadily, he replied, "No, I haven't fed yet."

"I wish I had known this. Tariq believed you would have fed on something by now. Why didn't you let anyone know this? I could have brought you a bag of plasma from our blood bank, or even a vial of Tariq's blood."

"I don't want human blood. I need to find an animal to feed on."

Rochelle laughed. She continued to laugh until her olive-skinned face was bright red. "That's stupid, Frank."

"What's so stupid about that?"

"I thought you were just a little smarter than that. We all just figured Norman would be the issue, not you. We have to feed on human blood. It's who we are. It's what we are."

"I don't care."

"You're never going to survive as a vampire this way. It's suicide. You should have just let that vampire hunting bitch finish you off when she took Norman out."

"I need to get to Marjorie. She'll be able to make it better. She's always been there to help see me through my problems."

Rochelle sighed. "She's not going to be able to help you out with this one. I don't even think you should go there, Frank. I believe we should get back in the car and head back to the facility. Tariq will know what to do."

"No." Frank got out of the car and began to back up away from Rochelle. "I'm not going back to that goddam prison!"

Rochelle tried to reason with him. "Now, come on Frank. It doesn't have to be like this. We can fix it together."

Frank turned back and ran towards the dark woods that surrounded the rest area. His pace was slow and unsteady. Rochelle chased after him and was easily able to catch up. She called out, "Frank! Frank, you're not in your right mind! Bloodthirst is taking control of you. So, come back to the car and we'll talk about this!"

Frank knelt down in the grass. "I don't want to come back to the car, Rochelle. I want to go into the woods and find animals to feed on. If I find a lot of them, I'll feel better."

Rochelle inched over and stood in front of him. With a threatening tone in her voice, Rochelle said, "I don't think so. There's only one option, and that's the facility."

Still kneeling down in the grass, Frank could feel danger all around him in the darkness, Rochelle being the most immediate danger. He had to find a way. He had to do something to get away from her. He grabbed a thick tree branch from the ground and jumped up. *That's it! A stake!* Rochelle saw the branch and shouted out, "No, Frank! This is not how it should be!"

In an instant, Frank plunged the branch into Rochelle's chest. The branch went in deep. *Take that, you lying bitch!*

Fascinated, he backed away from Rochelle and watched her body slowly combust into flames. He watched until Rochelle was reduced to nothing more than a pile of white ashes that would blow away with the first strong wind. *Rochelle was bad, but I got her before she got me. Oh God. I'll have to tell Norman about this. He'll get a laugh out of it. Oh, wait, Norman's gone.*

Then Frank made his way back to the car and sat for a moment, trying to get his bearings. He turned the key, backed out of the parking space and got back on the interstate to Boston. *It was her or me. There's no way that she was taking me back to that facility.*

•

Frank made his way into Boston just after midnight. He had pulled over along the highway a few times to regain some equilibrium and respite from his hallucinations. With every vehicle that passed him on the highway, he could only think of the driver and their throat. *Blood. All I want is warm delicious blood.*

The shock of murdering Rochelle and the increasing need to consume blood were taking a toll on him. He was sweating and shivering at the same time. His head was pounding hard. His stomach was weak. He wasn't well.

As he turned onto the street where his sister lived, he phoned Tariq. Frank informed him that he'd destroyed Rochelle. There was disappointment and anger in Tariq's voice. "Frank, vampires should not kill their own kind. We want the population of vampires to increase."

"I didn't have a choice. She wanted to bring me back to Collinsville and that wasn't what you promised would happen."

"This is not acceptable."

"I'm sorry, Tariq. I don't know what to do. I can't even see straight."

Angry, Tariq inquired, "You still have not fed on a human? What the hell is wrong with you, Frank? I thought you were smarter than that. I had higher hopes for you."

"I feel like I'm going to die. Every part of my body is shaking."

"I know where you are going. I am sending someone else to get you."

Frank realized and conceded to the fact that his place was back at the facility for now. "Yes. I'll see my sister and then you should come and take me back to be with you. I know you were right. I never should have left there in the first place. It was too soon and I didn't understand."

"Hold on, Frank."

"I'll try."

"No, Frank. Listen to me. Do not go into your sister's house. It is very dangerous. Hold on and wait in the car."

"Don't worry, Tariq. I know I'm safe with Marjorie. She won't hurt me." Frank ended the call as Tariq pleaded to an empty line.

Frank pulled into Marjorie's driveway. He stumbled out of the car and fell on the front lawn. Marjorie and her husband, Ted, heard the car as it pulled up. They came outside and saw Frank lying on the ground."

Marjorie shouted, "Frank! Oh God, there's something wrong with him."

After helping him back to his feet, the two of them put their arms around him and walked him into the house. As they walked, Frank looked into his sister's eyes and whispered, "Marjorie, I finally made it here."

Frank sat down on the sofa. He slumped and appeared as if he needed medical attention. Ted and Marjorie sat across the room. She questioned, "Do you need a doctor, Frank?"

He sounded exhausted when he said, "No. I don't need a doctor. That's not what I need. You'd never believe me if I told you." *I need to taste the warm blood of a human.*

"Then tell me where you've been for the last four weeks."

Frank tried to explain but it was a struggle to get the words out. "You're not going to believe me when I tell you. I was abducted."

"Abducted?"

"Kidnapped. I was held prisoner and kept in a dark basement."

Marjorie rushed to his side and sat beside him. "Oh Frank, what did they do to you? Did they hurt you?"

This was the part that Frank knew she would never believe. He realized how completely insane it would sound and that she might think he needed to see a shrink. "I was poisoned."

"They poisoned you? How did you get out of there?"

"I didn't. One minute I was in the basement Then, days later, I woke up in some kind of facility. It was like a hospital."

"Someone rescued you and took you to a hospital? That's good, Frank."

"No, Marjorie. It wasn't like that. No one came to rescue me." Frank struggled to remain in an upright position.

"But you just told me that you were in a hospital. How did you get from the basement to the hospital?"

Frank finally found the courage to blurt out the truth. "My kidnapper took me there. It wasn't a damned hospital. It was a facility. I didn't need to be in a hospital anymore. I was already dead. They killed me, Marjorie."

Marjorie looked over at her husband with a look of complete confusion. Then she wanted more clarity. She questioned Frank slowly, as if he were mentally impaired. "But, if they killed you, Frank, you couldn't be sitting here now. People can't still walk around if they're dead."

"Yes, I could. They brought me back from the dead. They injected me with vampire blood and changed me into one of them." Frank's breathing was getting shallow. The pain and bloodlust were devastating him.

Marjorie let out a quick giggle. "That's your story, Frank? After all this time and all the endless nights of worry, that's the best explanation that you can come up with?"

"It's all true."

"And where's this Rochelle woman you said was coming with you?"

"She's dead."

"Dead?"

"Yes, dead."

"How?"

"I killed her. Rochelle was a vampire and she tried to stop me from coming here, so I drove a tree branch into her heart."

Marjorie and Ted couldn't believe what was being said. "Frank, you're telling me that you're a vampire and you just killed another vampire on the way here?"

Frank was becoming more frustrated with Marjorie and the conversation. "It's all true. This is why I'm dying again. It's because I won't feed on a human being. And not feeding on human blood will eventually kill me."

Marjorie waved her hand in the air and said, "Oh Frank, this is crazy. There are no such things as vampires. They're just made-up characters to sell a bunch of books and movies."

Frantic over Frank's condition, Marjorie turned to Ted and began to talk to him about taking Frank to a hospital. Maybe Frank was strung out on drugs, or maybe someone really had poisoned him. It looked that way to her.

In his current state of mind, Frank could hear only jumbled bits and pieces of the discussion as he sat on the sofa and rocked back and forth. He vaguely heard "hospital" and thought that a hospital would be good – good for blood, bags and bags of blood. *Oh, sweet blood.*

Frank began to hallucinate in earnest. He saw and heard snippets of his dreams play out in vivid detail. Everything was jumbled and those damned spiders and bugs began to crawl over his skin again. He slapped at himself, trying to brush them off. Tariq was there, as well as the serpent with the tiny worthless legs. They hissed at him and laughed at him. The snake crawled inside Tariq's mouth and vanished in a flash of sparkling gems. Flapper girls stared at him with cold lifeless eyes. "Monster. Monster," they shouted at him while they smoked cigars and danced the Allemande. The red flames beckoned and laughed. He was in the desert and had blood dripping down his chin. It was thick and warm and Norman. Then, there was Norman. Oh God, Norman.

Just then, Marjorie and Ted noticed their children sitting on the stairs behind them, watching and listening to everything. They had told the kids that Uncle Frank was back and they had apparently been too excited to sleep. Ted gave the children a stern look, clapped his hands and said, "Aren't you both supposed to be in bed?"

Alice questioned, "Mom, what's wrong with Uncle Frank? He looks sick."

"He's not feeling well and you shouldn't be up this late."

"What's wrong with him?"

"That's none of your concern tonight, Alice. I want you both up in your beds by the time I count to ten."

Benny stood up and, before the countdown started, said, "I love you, Uncle Frank. Please get better soon."

"One, two, three …" But by the time the count was at three, Benny and Alice had gone back to the second floor and back to bed.

Frank pushed himself up from the sofa and walked across the room, looking as if he was drunk. He staggered around until he collapsed on top of Ted. Ted tried to push him off and Marjorie rushed over to pull him off. "Frank! Get off of Ted! What's wrong with you?"

But it was too late to help. Frank felt his razor-sharp vampire fangs emerge in his mouth and sink deep into Ted's throat. He tasted the warm delicious blood and felt the intense satisfaction that came along with it. *So good. So good. It's so warm and delicious.*

Marjorie was panic-stricken by now. She screamed and began to pound on Frank to pull him off Ted. "Get your hands off him! Frank, get off my husband!"

Frank didn't move. He was in a euphoric state, enjoying the taste and the warmth. *This is the most wonderful thing I've ever tasted.*

She shouted and pounded more. "Goddam it, get off him! Get off Ted!"

•

Frank opened his eyes. He found himself lying in a dark basement with a cold hard floor. He didn't feel sick anymore. He felt good. He felt like the old Frank, only better.

Not knowing how he had ended up in that basement, Frank sat up and looked around. He saw that there was a small window. He walked across the room and peeked out the window to see if it was day or night. "Nighttime. Thank God." He looked around at his surroundings for a moment and saw a set of stairs.

Frank strode to the wooden staircase and went up to the first floor. He was still in Marjorie's home. As he walked through the kitchen, he called out. "Marjorie, are you here? Ted! Benny! Alice! Is there anyone home?"

He entered the living room and saw Ted on the living room floor. There were bloodstains on the carpet all around him. He rushed across the room and knelt down next to Ted. "Ted? Can you hear me? What happened?" A terrible sense of dread began to seep into Frank. *Did I do this? No, I didn't do this. I could never do something like this. But I'm the only one here.*

He knew Ted was dead. Frank looked over to the dining room floor and saw Marjorie lying on her back with her throat torn open. *No! No! That's not Marjorie! Not my Marjorie.*

Frank tried to remember what happened to her. He couldn't. He could feel the tears as they welled up in his eyes. He looked at his favorite person in the world and felt the horror of what he saw. *It can't be.*

He whispered, "Oh no, Marjorie. Not you. Please, I couldn't have done this." He knelt over her, lifted her broken body in his arms and rocked back and forth. He wailed, "Come back … come back … come back."

His hysteria began to build. *The children. Benny and Alice.* He ran up the stairs to the second floor. He needed to know that the children were alright. Frank knew, if he had hurt the children, then he really was a monster.

He found Benny's body huddled up in the hallway. A look of fright and confusion was frozen on the boy's face. All the blood had been drained from his body.

He discovered Alice in her bed. She had been bitten and killed. Frank noticed that she was still hugging her teddy bear that was now covered with spatters of her blood.

Frank was filled with such self-loathing that he could barely breathe. He bent down to vomit, but nothing came up but fuzzy red bubbles. A wave of dizziness forced him to slump down against the wall for support.

Coherent thought escaped him. If he hadn't died already, he thought wildly, this is what it's really like to die. He was trapped in a frightening nightmare. But as much as he tried, he couldn't wake up from it. *Who did this to my family? Who would kill my family? Was it Rochelle? No, I killed Rochelle. Norman couldn't have done it. I didn't do this. Did I?*

His vision narrowed into a small black hole surrounded by a red mist, but he couldn't change the images that were right before his eyes. They were all dead. His family had been slaughtered and left there like old trash.

He began to scream and wail and make guttural sounds. He could feel his face contort and tears spill from his eyes. He continued to wail. The emotional pain was so great, he felt as if a brick had landed on his heart. The pain paralyzed him. *Dear God, what have I done?*

As his shock and horror slowly receded, for it did not go away, an unbearable sadness set in. He couldn't escape what he had done. He had resisted feeding on humans only to massacre the only four people on earth he truly cared about and that cared about him. Numbly, he thought, I have become a monster. *They were right. All of them were right. I am a monster.*

As he walked sluggishly back down the steps to the first floor, his phone rang. "Hello," he said listlessly.

Frank expected to hear Tariq's voice on the line. "Frank, it's Cassie."

Frank stopped dead in his tracks. "Cassie? Is that really you?" *Oh, I love the sound of your voice. It comforts me.*

"Yes. It's really me."

"I don't understand. Why are you calling me instead of Tariq?"

"I called to let you know that I'm on my way. I just arrived in Boston and I need directions to your location."

"Why are you here in Boston, Cassie?" *Why would Tariq send Cassie?*

"I'm the field man that Tariq sent to bring you back to the facility."

"You?"

"Yes me, Frank. Just because I'm level two doesn't mean that I can't get things done. Besides, I miss seeing your face."

Frank replied dully. "I miss seeing your face too, Cassie. I miss looking into your eyes. I miss so many things about you."

"What's wrong with your voice, Frank? You sound awful."

Frank knew that confession was good for the soul, but then, he didn't have a soul anymore. Did he? *I'm awful. I am truly a repulsive and loathsome monster.* "I just slaughtered my entire family. My sister, Marjorie, her husband and their two children are all dead."

"Why would you do that?"

"I don't know why I did it. I hadn't fed since I left the facility and ..."

"You never fed on a human? You must have been ravenous."

"I was. I was starving. But I don't remember doing any of this. And now, they're dead and I can't do a thing to change that." He moaned and sobbed uncontrollably.

"I'm so sorry, Frank. I know how much you loved your sister."

"My sister. Yes, my sister Marjorie."

"It wasn't your fault, Frank."

"Wasn't it?"

"You couldn't have known what would take place if you didn't feed."

"But I did know. Tariq told me this. I just chose to ignore him."

"Stop blaming yourself."

Frank tried to clear his throat and red mucus drained from his nose as he continued to sob. He knew that the only way forward for him was to bring Cassie to the house so she could return him to

Tariq. "If I give you the address, do you have a GPS to type it into?"

"I have the GPS on my phone."

"The address is 66 Lost Bridge Avenue. It's on the north side of the city."

Frank waited for her to type the address in the GPS. "Okay, Frank, it says I should be there in about fifteen minutes."

"I'll see you then." Frank hung up and went back into the living room and sat down on the sofa. He looked over at Ted's body again. Then he forced himself to stare at Marjorie's poor crumpled body. *I am not that man. I was never that kind of man. All life was important to me before this happened. He made me into this thing I never wanted to become. Tariq did this.* He wept.

Frank gazed at the stairs that led up to the second floor. *And those poor children. Defenseless young children staring into the eyes of the uncle that they trusted and loved.* Then, he stared at his sister's body again and contemplated. *What kind of terror did she feel while I murdered her? Did she try to fight back? Of course, she fought back. Did she beg me for mercy, my proud Marjorie?* He wept some more.

As he mourned what he had done to his family, he went to the closet for some blankets. He straightened the bodies and covered them, taking extra care with the children.

As he covered the body of his sister, he ran his hand across her sleek black hair one last time. *I love you, Marjorie. I always have. This life has no meaning without you.*

•

Fifteen minutes later, there was a quick tapping on the door accompanied by a kind voice. "Frank, I'm here." Frank didn't come to the door to greet her.

Cassie entered the dark house and, with her night vision, saw the covered bodies on the first floor. Then, she saw Frank who was still sitting on the sofa, trapped in his gut-wrenching grief. Cassie approached him.

"Hello, Cassie."

She walked over and hugged Frank. "I got here as fast as I could. You didn't sound too good when we spoke."

"Oh Cassie, how the hell could I have done this to my own family … and never remember any of it?" *But I know it was me.*

Cassie felt sympathy, but she couldn't keep the frustration out of her voice. "You don't want to remember it, Frank. Tariq explained to you that when a vampire doesn't feed, he becomes weak and he hallucinates. The absence of human blood will eventually make a vampire reach the tipping point between sanity and psychosis. I believe you were at that point. Why didn't you just listen to the man and stay with us at the facility a little longer? It would have changed so many things."

"I don't know why I didn't stay. I guess it was because I didn't believe what I had become. I was a fool."

Cassie smiled sadly at Frank and nodded. "Yes, you were. I know that those are harsh words but they're the truth. If you had just stayed when we asked you to, your sister and her children would still be alive, and Norman and Rochelle would still be with us."

He stared deeply into her brilliant eyes and said, "Cassie, I want you to do something for me. I need you to do it."

"What would that be, Frank?"

"I know this is asking a lot from you but, I want you to kill me."

"For God's sake, Frank, I can't do that! I would never kill you. You're just in shock. You'll get over it."

"Just kill me here, Cassie, so Tariq doesn't do it. Tell him I went crazy and left you no choice but to finish me off."

"No, Frank."

He insisted, "I can't live with myself and I want you to end my miserable life. You are the closest thing to a friend that I have left in this world. Please, Cassie?"

Cassie grabbed Frank's hand and spoke to him intently. "Frank, now you listen to me. This kind of thing has happened before and will happen again. Tariq is upset but he's not going to end you and neither will I. Just come back with me and you can get help that will ease your pain. In time, if you still feel the same way, we'll talk about this again. Besides that, Frank, we have a future together, you and I. Do you hear me, Frank? Will you please trust me on this?"

Frank gazed at Cassie for a long time, then nodded dully. "Do I have a choice?" *My choices are few and far between these days.*

"No, Frank."

"So, what do we do now?"

Cassie rattled her keys and said, "We get the hell out of here now."

"But what about the bodies? Don't we have to clean them up and bury them so they won't be discovered?"

Cassie rolled her shoulders and grinned. "I think you watch too many of those cheap b-movies, Frank. We're not going to clean up a damned thing in here. It's not necessary. We're getting in the car and heading back to Collinsville before someone finds us."

"Someone? You mean one of those goddam vampire hunters?" *Oh yeah. Karen, that bitch. I forgot all about her.*

"That's exactly who I'm talking about. Now, let's get going now, Frank."

Just as Cassie turned around and faced the door, she heard a voice. "Come out, come out, wherever you are ... I know you're in there, so come out or I'm coming in."

Frank knew that voice. *How the hell was Karen able to find me?* Then, he remembered the time they spent together in that filthy basement. "I told her all about my sister, Marjorie. I told her they lived in Boston. I think, at one point, I even told her Marjorie's last name was Cooper." *Goddam! How could I have been so stupid? I practically handed her a roadmap.*

Cassie rolled her eyes. "You're a real piece of work, Frank. A real piece of work. Why didn't you just send her an invite?"

They heard the sound of glass smashing somewhere on the first floor. Frank and Cassie raced around to find out which window had been broken.

They stopped when they got to the kitchen and saw Karen standing there next to the sink. She was holding a cross in one hand and a wooden stake in the other hand. "I told you to come outside or I was coming in."

Frank asked, "Why are you doing this to me, Karen? I never hurt you. In fact, I was the one who wanted to save you."

She shook her head. "No, it's true You never hurt me. Where is your sister?"

Frank lowered his head. "She's gone."

"And the children and her husband? Where are they?"

"All gone."

"You see, you never hurt me but your sister and her family aren't here anymore. Those wicked creatures back in Collinsville turned you into this monster, Frank."

Frank looked at Cassie and then lowered his head and stared at the kitchen floor. "I'm not proud of what I did. I am a monster."

"And you did it, Frank. You committed the crime. You actually murdered your own niece and nephew, two innocent children who didn't deserve to die. What does that make you? You're no better than the rest of them."

Frank whispered, "I already know what I am. I'm a cold-blooded killer."

Cassie elbowed Frank and, in a low voice, said, "Don't listen to her, Frank. She's one of those filthy vampire hunters, which makes her no better than us."

Frank stood there, still dazed and confused over what he had done to his sister, her children, her family. He didn't think of Cassie as being evil. No, not at all. He didn't even think Karen was evil. Not really. Frank's judgement was focused solely on himself and what he had done. Things he thought he wasn't capable of doing. Things that made him dark and evil. "Isn't this what Karen is supposed to do, Cassie, kill those who kill others?"

Cassie tried to snap Frank out of his guilt-ridden stupor. "She was groomed to kill from the moment she could walk. Her children are being groomed for the same thing. We can't let her win this fight, Frank."

Karen inched closer to Frank and told him, "The major difference between the vampire and the vampire hunter is that I don't slaughter the innocent ones. That's what you do. I only kill those who are deserving of death and, right now, you both meet the qualifications."

Frank knew he was guilty of committing the vilest sin possible. "I know that what I did is … is unforgivable in the eyes of God." He lifted his head up. "But I don't remember doing it. Shouldn't that count for something?"

Karen snickered. "Jesus Christ, Frank, didn't those idiots teach you anything back in Collinsville? Even I know that the bloodlust can throw a vampire into a hysterical frenzy."

Cassie, who had been studying the hunter all along, pulled her shoulders back and stood up tall.

She drew a pair of gloves from her pocket and put them on. She'd had enough of Karen and her trivial vampire analysis. "I suppose you should shut up and do what you came here to do then … or at least try to."

Karen moved closer. Instinctively, Frank backed away from her, then steeled himself and held his ground. Cassie moved away from the two of them and stood in an attack position. Karen tossed a crucifix towards Cassie. When it hit her in the chest, Cassie let out a tiny yelp. Instantly, she was paralyzed as she fell down on the floor, staring up at Karen and Frank.

Karen walked with great confidence across the kitchen towards Frank, wooden stake in hand. Frank saw the murderous look in her eyes and quickly understood what Cassie had said about the hunters. They were no better than the vampires. When she got close to him, she whispered, venom dripping from her voice, "Trust me, Frank. This is only going to hurt for a second."

Frank was ready to go. He knew he was a murderer and deserved to die. He'd never wanted to be a vampire anyway. The bad luck of being in the wrong place at the right time had let him down and Tariq had made the choice for him. "I'm not going to fight you, Karen. I want to die as much as you want to kill me. Funny. Maybe we'll meet again in hell one day."

Cassie was a strong and capable vampire and managed to sit up as she regained her strength quickly. But she was still shaking off the effects of the crucifix as she watched helplessly when Karen took aim, lunged at Frank and drove the wooden stake into his heart.

"Oh God, Frank!"

The women watched as Frank's body began to combust. He screamed out with intense pain and ran into the dining room. Karen, feeling boundless pleasure when watching a vampire die, trailed him there to watch him careen around the room, bounce off the curtains and the furniture, and light the house on fire. And then, he stopped moving as he became dark gray ashes that rained down upon his sister's body.

Karen knew that the entire house would eventually burn down to the foundation. She also knew she had one more vampire to destroy before her work there was finished.

As she walked cautiously back into the kitchen, Cassie was no longer sitting on the floor. Karen knew that Cassie was still somewhere in the house. When she turned to go back to the living room, she gasped when she saw Cassie lurking right behind her.

And though the flames were spreading fast, Karen yanked another wooden stake from her jacket pocket. She held it up in front of Cassie and said, "I have one more job to do tonight. Then, I'm going home to my children."

Cassie didn't say a word. Her confidence equaled Karen's. They dove at each other with great force while the flames climbed the staircase to the second floor.

•

Karen opened her eyes and found that she was in complete darkness. She tried to move but her body was weak. She was experiencing intense pain in her stomach and her throat. She tried to shout out but her mouth was as dry as sandpaper. "Is there anyone there?"

She swallowed over and over to create some moisture in her mouth. The pain in her throat was intense. She didn't know where she was or how she'd gotten there. She'd been in a place like this before. "Is there anyone out there who can help me? Frank, can you hear me? Frank?"

She heard nothing. She realized she must be the only one in the room. Karen tried to roll over but couldn't. The pain throughout her body was overwhelming.

She thought back to the last thing she could remember. Suddenly, she remembered, she'd killed Frank! The house had caught fire. She'd held up the wooden stake and lunged at Cassie. Then … then … had she destroyed Cassie?

Karen heard a door opening and closing. She heard the squishing sound of shoes on the tile floor as the person came closer to her. She tried to see a face but it was too dark and she couldn't yet focus. She whispered, "I'm in extreme pain, my throat, my stomach. Where am I?"

"Why, you've been here in Collinsville for a few weeks, Karen."

Karen recognized the voice. She knew then that she hadn't killed the vampire. Cassie was still alive and standing in the room right next to her bed. "Cassie? Cassie?"

"Yes. It's me."

In a low whisper, she said disappointingly, "Back at the house, I was confident that I staked you. I suppose you didn't die."

With a perky tone, Cassie replied, "Nope, I didn't die, sweetie … but you sure did." Cassie came around the bed and stood where Karen could see now that her eyes finally began to focus. Cassie was not wearing a mask.

Karen gasped when she realized she was there to be turned into a vampire. "No, you can't do this to me. In all of history, no vampire hunter has ever been turned."

"Then, I suppose you'll be the first, Karen. Now do be quiet so I can give you your shot." She took a glass syringe from her pocket and popped the plastic cap onto the floor.

Karen begged her, "Please don't do this to me, Cassie."

"Oh, it's happening and you have no choice in the matter."

"Please don't."

"I have to say, Karen, Tariq was devastated when you destroyed his darling Frank, and Norman too. And yet, I've never seen the man happier to be changing someone into a vampire. He's practically wetting himself knowing that the hunter has become the hunted. It took me from level two to level five in one day. He's so proud."

Karen cringed, knowing she had lost and the vampires had won.

"Tariq and I have such wonderful plans for you, Karen. It's a whole new world … just for you. We looked forward to our future with Frank. Well, I did especially, but since he's no longer here, you'll just have to do."

Cassie played with the amulet around her neck, the one she had snatched from Karen's neck before she'd overpowered her in the burning house that night. "I have your lovely amulet."

Karen suddenly knew why Cassie had put the gloves on that night.

Cassie was wise enough and calculated enough to protect herself from the silver chain. New vampires wouldn't know that taking away a hunter's talisman weakened them, but Cassie knew. She had been a vampire for decades now and, unlike Frank or Norman, she'd taken the time and had the patience to learn how to defend herself against the hunters.

Cassie's feminine loveliness masked her cunning and strength. And, although she formed loving attachments, as she had with Frank, she had a vengeful streak that revealed itself to those who wronged her.

Karen laid there for a moment, staring at Cassie's form. She was stunned. "Why? Why?" She questioned stupidly.

"Why not?" There was a long pause before Cassie continued. "By the way, your children are here at the facility."

Nervously, Karen asked, "What? You have my children here?"

"Yes, I do."

Karen was gradually fading but still begged, "But they're just two innocents. Please, don't hurt my children."

"No. We'd never dream of hurting them. In fact, they're quite the little darlings around here. They have a great time playing the vampire hunter game with Glenn and Wayne. Did you teach them that, Karen?"

Karen began to babble. "No, I didn't teach them anything like that. They're much too young to learn about becoming hunters." She begged, "Do whatever you want to do with me, but please don't hurt my children. Please, don't hurt them." Cassie crossed her arms and rolled her eyes.

"Very well put, Karen. We'll do what we have to do. That's kind of how we felt too. You see, we're already thinking alike. Now, what's going to happen is that once you've been turned into a full-fledged vampire, we decided … well … I decided that we're going to starve you. No human blood for Karen."

"Why would you do that?"

"Because we know how much you abhor the consumption of human blood. After all, that's why you kill us, isn't it? We know that your thirst will build and build into a frenzy, like it did with Frank, and all you'll be able to think about is the taste of human blood, the warm and comforting feeling of it entering your body."

Karen listened, but was so mortified, she couldn't speak.

"But you already knew that, right, Karen? You laughed and taunted Frank for succumbing to his bloodlust and killing his family."

Cassie leaned down and tweaked Karen's nose. Cassie was burning with delight to finish her story. "But here's the best part of all. Once you're ravenous and hallucinating, we're going to secure you in a very nice room on the fourth floor and let your sweet children come in to visit you. We want to make it comfortable for them, you see. Never let it be said that we mistreated your children. It should be quite a reunion."

Karen pleaded, wild eyed, "You can't do that. You know I won't be strong enough to hold back and I'll end up killing them."

Cassie clapped her hands and smiled. "And that will take care of another pathetic generation of vampire hunters."

Cassie stared into Karen's eyes when she caressed her cheek, taking satisfaction in knowing that the woman who wanted to destroy her was about to enter her dark and sinister world. "I think you said it best to Frank just before you murdered him. This is only going to hurt for a second." She laughed as she plunged the syringe into Karen's arm and watched the terror on her face.

Karen's thoughts came crashing down and spun in an endless circle, "The children, the other hunters, Cassie, Frank, Norman …"

As Karen drifted into fitful sleep, she heard another voice say, "Maybe we'll meet again in hell one day."

Made in the USA
Middletown, DE
09 January 2022

58222667R00151